Praise for *Down Went Alice*

"From page one, Kristen Skeet successfully grabbed me and took me on a fast-paced trip through the twists and turns of Alice's childhood...Alice's diary brought me right into her world of fame and misfortune and kept me there until the very end."

—Lynn M. Lombard, Writer, Akron, New York

"Kristen Skeet's novel "had me" with the Introduction and I never stopped turning pages until her last word. Exceptional storytelling, compelling characters, believable situations, terrific pacing...I want more from this author and hope she considers telling me what happens next in the life of Alice Moriarty. "

—Terri Skurzewski, Elma, New York, Co-Author of *No Stoppin' This Boppin'*

"*Down Went Alice* by Kristen Skeet is a moving and starkly poignant story that is masterfully told...bringing you inside Alice's head. You hear all the voices there, feel the emotions, sense the underlying fears and demons. When an author can do that...it is magic.

—Linda Lou Weaver Oliphant, Reader, Santa Teresa, New Mexico

"Follow Alice down the rabbit hole! The rollercoaster ride of drugs, sex, rock 'n roll and the people it destroys is a fascinating read. Alice's sardonic, sometimes hilarious insights...make for a book that you can't put down!"

—Sherry McCutcheon, Reader, Athens, Georgia

Down Went Alice

To the loving memory of Craig Pixley.

You are loved and missed every day.

Down Went Alice

The Diary of Alice Moriarty

Kristen Skeet

ISBN-13: 978-0-692-73584-8 (Kristen Skeet)

ISBN-10: 0692735844

Cover art by Michaela Stejskalova/Shutterstock

Cover design by Katie Zaharkin
k86c@yahoo.com

Edited by Nancy Eckerson, Write Now! Inc.
www.nancyeckerson.com

Author photograph by Emma Grace Masternak

Published by: Kristen Skeet
www.kristenskeet.com

Table of Contents

"In another moment down went Alice after it, never once considering how in the world she was to get out again."

—Lewis Carroll, *Alice's Adventures in Wonderland*

Acknowledgements

A sincere and heartfelt thank you to: Debbie Skeet and Roger Skeet for being my parents and for allowing my imagination to roam free; Stephanie Masternak for being my sister and for your cool head through the gauntlet of every "Exact Change Only" toll booth; Jim Barron for humoring my incessant traveling and for supporting me in everything I've done these last eleven years; Sherry McCutcheon for being my sounding board. You were the first person I told about this story, and you immediately encouraged me to get it down on paper. Your friendship means the world to me; Tuesday night writer's group: Nancy Eckerson, Lynn Lombard, Jessie Miller and Terri Skurzewski for welcoming me into your group and for offering me your input and encouragement without reservation; Katie Zaharkin for your amazing cover design; Emma Grace Masternak for your beautiful photography; Abby Masternak for your outstanding "try not to giggle so much" NYC advice; Nancy Eckerson, for your painstaking editing; and, of course, Mr. Charles Dodgson, pen name Lewis Carroll, for writing *Alice's Adventures in Wonderland*. Without it, my story wouldn't exist.

INTRODUCTION

Rock stars, Stephen Moriarty, Alfie Evans, and Stuart Townsend grew up together in the seaside town of Blackpool in North West England. As young men, the boys formed a rock band that enjoyed a large, local following, but desiring fame and fortune, the teenagers migrated to Los Angeles together in 1973. There they toiled in musical oblivion for three years before singer, Sara Adams, came along.

Alfie and Sara were inseparable from the moment they met on the Sunset Strip in 1976. They loved each other deeply, loved each other to the point of obsession, some said. Soon, the boys invited Sara to join their band, and it was with that decision they became *Wonderland*.

Within a month, *Wonderland* was signed to a record deal. Three months later, they released their first album, and inside of six months, they embarked on their first world tour.

Their success was greater than any of them could have imagined. For nearly a decade, they recorded wildly successful albums and toured the world behind them.

But something went terribly wrong. During the year-long world tour for their fifth album, at the highest peak of their success, Alfie walked away from Sara and *Wonderland*, vowing never to return. This came after an infamous fight backstage between Alfie and Stephen, during which Stephen revealed his affair with Sara, and that she was pregnant with his child.

I am that child.

My existence has haunted me my entire fucking life.

You see, it's not something you can get used to: the surprise on your own mother's face every time she looks at you. Her confusion. Like she thought you were part of some horrible nightmare she'd had; that you should have been gone by morning's light.

Still. I loved her.

I loved her as much as she loved her fans; as much as they loved her.

As much as she loved him.

Alfie.

Alfie *fucking* Evans.

The bane of my inconvenient existence.

It was because of Alfie she invited these men into her life. There were many of them over the years. The very best one was *Wonderland* manager, and my one-time stepfather, Jett Andrews. The worst of the lot was...well, you'll have no trouble figuring that one out.

My name is Alice, and this is my story of *Wonderland*.

PART ONE:
THE BEGINNING

TOUGH LITTLE ALICE

The night before my fifteenth birthday, Sara's live-in boyfriend, Chuck Wall, appeared at my bedroom door. He was dressed only in jeans and they were slung low around his hips. Dangerously low. Disgustingly low.

I can't imagine Jett having walked around the house like that back when he and Sara were still married. Not at all, really, but certainly not while I was around.

I ignored Chuck that night, hoping he would just go away, but of course he didn't.

"Are you excited for your party?" he asked.

Chuck was from somewhere in England. I don't know which part. I didn't ask. I didn't fucking care. His accent was different from Stephen's and Stuart's, so I knew he wasn't from Blackpool, but that's about as much thought as I gave it. He sounded sophisticated and polite when he talked, though—a direct contradiction to the thoughts in his head.

"My party?" I asked.

"Your birthday party, tomorrow," he said.

Ah, yes, of course.

Apparently, the party the next night was a celebration, in honor of my birthday, but the charade was ridiculous. If those two had really wanted to do something nice for me for my birthday, they would have postponed the partying for a night and let me get some sleep for a change.

"Fifteen already..." said Chuck. "Where does the time go?"

"Oh, I don't know," I said, looking at him. "Up your nose with everything else?"

The eye contact was a bad idea. I think he thought I was flirting with him, because he smiled and rubbed his belly. This lowered his jeans even more, and my eyes drifted involuntarily to the dark patch of hair that disappeared beneath his waistband. I looked away quickly, disgusted with myself, but his slow smile told me he hadn't missed it.

Chuck had lived at the house for about five years at that point, and for the first few years, we just kind of ignored each other. He didn't seem to want anything to do with me, and I certainly didn't want anything to do with him. I was just his girlfriend's annoying kid. Sara felt no need to make me a priority in her life, so it wasn't like he had to suck up to me to stay close to her. Actually, that's probably why she kept him around—he was as uninterested in me as she was.

It was only that previous year or so he really started taking a liking to me. It was right around the time I stopped looking like a little girl and started looking like a woman, give or take. He loitered near me more and more everyday that year, it seemed. As if puberty wasn't horrifying enough.

"You look older than fifteen," he said, right on cue.

I set my guitar down long enough to grab a cigarette and lit it, expelling the smoke forcefully from my mouth.

"Does your mother know you smoke?"

"Who knows?" I said.

"And your father?"

"My father knows very little about me," I said.

As you well know, dickhead.

"Does that make you sad?" asked Chuck.

"No."

"Tough, little Alice," he cooed.

Cigarette between my lips, I played some more, waiting for him to give up and leave.

"You're very talented," he said. "No surprise there, considering your parents."

I ignored him and continued to strum.

"Maybe you and I can do an album together someday," he said. "I'm a hit maker, Alice."

Chuck was a record producer, and an acclaimed one at that, unfortunately. He was the man responsible for much of *Wonderland's* success and most of Sara's success as a solo artist. "The man behind the music," they called him.

Sure, there were the rumors about his rampant drug use and many sexual indiscretions, but what are a few felonies compared to hundreds of millions of dollars? A man can be forgiven for just about anything with that much money at stake.

I clamped down on the strings, and the guitar was silent. I looked sidelong at Chuck, careful not to make eye contact this time.

"You're a creep and a fraud," I said. "And everybody knows it."

In my peripheral, he smirked. It was the smirk of a man who knew his place in that house—and my life—was solid, and he wasn't wrong. Sara was completely dependent on Chuck by then; hooked on the drugs he gave her. She would do anything to keep him around. She would turn a blind eye to anything for one more hit.

Speaking of the devil, Sara appeared then, dressed in a glamorous gown. They were off to some fancy industry event, not that they had told me about it. Jett was the one who had told me. He'd stopped by earlier that day on his way to the dry cleaners to pick up his "monkey suit," as he put it, and had bellyached to me about having to attend.

"Do you have..." said Sara.

She froze when she saw me. It was my bedroom and had been for almost fifteen years, yet she was surprised to find me in it. She was always so fucking surprised to see me.

"What are you doing?" Sara asked Chuck.

He didn't bother to wipe the smirk from his face, digging into his pocket. He pulled out a bottle of pills and handed it to her. "I'm just chatting with our girl here."

Sara took in his state of undress, and, for a moment, for one hopeful moment, I thought she might yell at him.

"The limo will be here in ten minutes," she said.

"I'll be ready," he said.

She left without another glance in my direction.

Mother of the year, ladies and gentlemen.

Chuck waited a few seconds and then crossed the room, crouching by my bed. He put his arms on either side of me. "Not everybody knows it, love."

I stared hard at my bedspread, refusing to react to him.

He scoffed. "You should loosen up, kid." He straightened and patted my leg. "If you want something stronger than a cigarette tomorrow, find me. It's your day, after all."

As soon as he was gone, I ran into my bathroom and threw up. I rinsed my mouth out and looked at my reflection, shocked by the gaunt, pale creature staring back at me. I'd always had an uncanny resemblance to Sara, but thanks to the near-constant anxiety, courtesy of Chuck, I'd started to resemble the drug-addicted version of her she'd become.

I decided then I would do something. I didn't know yet what it would be, but I knew something had to be done, and I knew it would be me doing it. Sara certainly wasn't going to help. Stephen wasn't sober long enough to have any sort of meaningful conversation with. Jett would've helped, but Jett had already done so much for me, and I wasn't his responsibility anymore.

Somehow, one way or another, Chuck Wall would be out of that house, and soon.

I should have known better, Diary.

IT'LL COST YOU

Early the next afternoon, I was in the kitchen searching for something to eat. Well, I was in one of the kitchens of that house, I should say. Sara's house was a sprawling fourteen-bedroom, twenty-three bathroom monstrosity with three guest houses, a full movie theatre and five kitchens.

Twenty-three bathrooms!

Who the fuck needs twenty-three bathrooms?

Rock stars and their druggie friends, that's who. The folks of Sodom and Gomorrah had nothing on Sara and her revolving collection of "yes" people. Rumor has it God once tried to destroy them by raining down salt and sulfur, but those fuckers just snorted it all up and continued on with their debauchery.

Okay, that last part was a fib, but the parties at Sara's house were legendary, and they would have slid seamlessly into that biblical tale.

The after-party for whatever the hell event they'd gone to the night before was no different. It had raged well into the morning, as usual. Stragglers were sprawled throughout the house, again. There'd been one of them on my bathroom floor when I got up to pee. That charmer was passed out in his own vomit with his fly wide open, and his flaccid, little willy peeking out.

Ah, memories.

Nothing about that house ever felt like a home to me. It was cavernous and cold and uninviting. Like a museum: all marble and columns. There were two life-sized statues in the foyer, on either side of the staircase, and they terrified me when I was a kid. I used to imagine them coming to life and chasing me up the stairs, but I soon learned that the real monsters are people. Before long, those statues became my imagined protectors and friends.

That morning, I assumed the drugged-up, dynamic duo were still asleep (they rarely got out of bed before dusk) and went in search of food. Finding an empty pantry and nearly empty fridge, I went to the wet bar in the Great Room and fixed myself a birthday drink instead. I lit a cigarette, held the still-lit match over the whiskey, and wished that Chuck Wall would just go the fuck away.

(Yes, I was a regular drinker of whiskey by age fifteen, which might sound bad, but I was actually eight the first time I had it. Stuart let me have some of his. It burned so badly that I gagged and spit it out and didn't go near the stuff again for years. That was his plan, I'm sure. I was the ripe, old age of thirteen by the time I made my way back to the whiskey. By then, the burn was a welcome diversion.

Lovely Stuart. *Wonderland* drummer, Stuart Townsend somehow came off as the most responsible of those from the band (forget I just told you he let an eight-year-old drink whiskey), and I'm not sure how. That's rare for a drummer, isn't it? He was also fun and never creepy. He'd never banged Sara just because he probably could have if he'd asked nicely. I guess you could call him the gentlemen of the group.)

There came a shuffling behind me as I blew out the birthday match. I thought one of the stragglers had come foraging for food, so I did the shot and collected the bottle to clear out of there.

"Happy birthday," said Sara.

I spun around and, realizing it was her, shoved the bottle behind me on instinct. After all, most mothers would be upset to find their teenage daughter chugging whiskey for breakfast.

"Don't look so surprised," she said.

But my surprise was impossible to hide, and it was three-fold. I was not only surprised she was awake already, or that she remembered it was my birthday, but her appearance was alarming as well. Her hair was limp and lifeless, and the circles under her eyes were as dark as her brown eyes. Her collarbone and sternum jutted out of her skin at the opening of her black, silk robe that was tied loosely around her minuscule waist.

She was wasting away.

Chuck was killing her.

"You don't have to hide that," said Sara, gesturing to the bottle. "We know you drink."

Sara had become incapable of referring to herself in the singular by that point. Everything was "we" or "us" when it came to Chuck. It drove me nuts. I wanted to smack her every time she did it.

Sara had been fiercely independent in the early days of *Wonderland*. She was only seventeen when she joined and had already been living on her own for quite a while. I never knew my grandparents—either set— but, from what I've read, Sara's parents weren't at all supportive of her musical aspirations, so she left the house at sixteen and never looked back.

Thirty plus years later, she couldn't make it through a day without a pill or a man to prop her up. How the hell had that happened?

I set the bottle on top of the white, baby grand piano by the bar and poured myself another one.

"Pour me one too?" asked Sara, sitting behind the keys.

"Shouldn't you have coffee or breakfast or something first?"

"Shouldn't you?" she countered.

"I've been up for hours," I lied. "And I have eaten."

"I'm not hungry," she said.

"You should eat something."

"I said I'm not hungry."

I considered another moment and then shrugged. I poured her a drink and slid it to her, grabbing a second glass for myself.

We sipped our drinks—Sara on one side of the piano and me on the other. It might as well have been an island between us for all the distance I felt. We were like old classmates who had gotten together for brunch and realized they had absolutely nothing to talk about.

"Thank you," I said finally.

"For?"

"The happy birthday."

"Sure," she said, nodding.

She set her drink down and her fingers sprinkled over the keys, creating a beautiful tune, but she soon stopped. The drugs squashed her creative spark. The only time Chuck backed off on giving them to her was when it was time for her to be creative and make money for him—when it was time for a new album or tour.

She stared at the keys and, after a long pause, she said, "Can I ask you something?"

"Sure."

"Why do you live here?" she asked, picking up her drink again.

I wasn't prepared for that one.

"What do you mean?" I asked.

"This isn't the best place in the world for a kid."

Her moment of self-awareness stunned me.

"Well, I'm not really a kid," I said.

Not anymore.

"You know what I mean," she said.

"I'm not sure I do," I said.

Sara sighed, swirling the whiskey in her glass.

"Where else would I go?" I prompted.

"Stephen would take you."

Stephen would take you.

My father, *Wonderland* bassist, Stephen Moriarty, lived in a cozy, little six-bedroom, seven-bath mansion about a mile down the winding road.

I had often wondered why I lived with Sara and not with him. They gave me his last name, after all. So, why did I live with her?

I suppose it was because he didn't want me there. Not full time, anyhow. Live-in daughters and long-term groupies don't mix so well, you see.

"He doesn't want me," I said.

"We're all doing things we don't want, aren't we?" she said.

I set my drink down. "Are you asking me to move out?"

"No, I just...I don't know," said Sara. "Forget it."

Not likely.

Sara had never been thrilled to have me around, but she'd tolerated me well enough for fifteen years. It made no sense that she would be broaching that subject then.

It didn't seem likely, but I wondered if Sara had finally caught on to Chuck's lewd behavior. Was she trying to get me to leave the house for my own good?

I was about to ask her when he wandered into the Great Room, robed for once, thankfully.

"Good morning, ladies," said Chuck.

I kept my eyes on Sara. "It's afternoon."

Chuck leaned between us to kiss Sara and then turned to me, gripping my chin. "Happy birthday, Little One."

I slapped his hand away. "Don't touch me."

He whooped, slapping the counter top. "You've got some fire in you, girl."

"I don't like being touched."

"Maybe nobody's ever touched you right," said Chuck.

I waited for Sara to say something, anything, but she said nothing. It was then when I finally realized she would always say nothing to him about me.

"I left a treat for you on your nightstand, baby," said Chuck.

Sara got up and shuffled away like a goddamn zombie, leaving me alone with him.

It was then or never, in my mind. I knew what Chuck wanted from me, and I knew I could use it against him to finally nail him to the wall.

Mind made up, I stepped around him and swallowed the rest of my drink and, with it, the rage creeping up my throat. I leaned against the bar and looked up at him, trusting I was coming across as something resembling sexy.

"Maybe you're right," I said.

His features shifted into a mixture of surprise and amusement. "Oh?"

"Maybe it's time I loosened up a bit," I said. "Your offer still good?"

He leaned closer. His breath reeked of stale cigarettes, booze, and something rotten. "Which offer is that?"

"The something stronger," I said.

"That offer's always good." He tapped my nose with his finger. "It'll cost you though."

He hadn't meant money.

He watched for my reaction with perverted eyes. My hand rested only inches from a knife block on the bar. I fantasized about ripping out one of the blades and jamming it into his stomach over and over again until he stopped moving.

Perhaps he misinterpreted my grinning about the fantasy as excitement at his statement, because he smiled back.

Whiskey makes me ballsy, Diary. I pressed up on my tiptoes and touched my lips to his.

He drew in a quick breath and reeled back slightly, putting his hands on my shoulders. I stayed on tiptoe and gazed at his lips and then up into his eyes. He stared down at me, eyebrows furrowed. When I brushed my lips to his again, he dropped his hands and leaned into me.

That's when I knew I had him.

Someone made a racket out in the foyer. Maybe Sara. Maybe a straggler. Chuck backed away, his eyes trained on the entrance to the room.

"Tonight, then?" I asked. "Something stronger?"

He said nothing, but nodded, and then left the room, stumbling on an ottoman on his way out.

It was the first time I'd ever seen him unnerved.

I liked it.

BE CAREFUL WHAT YOU WISH FOR

Later that night, Chuck taunted Sara with a bottle of pills, dangling it over her head. Sara was on a doctor prescribed diet of anti-anxiety and depression meds, but Chuck had taken it upon himself to be her pharmacist, dispensing her pills as he saw fit.

Chuck instructed Sara to do a little twirl and then bow for the audience he'd amassed, the other assholes at the party. They hooted and hollered at her like she was the night's entertainment in a gentlemen's club. Not that they were gentlemen. They were scum. She wasn't safe from the vultures in her own home anymore.

I glared at Chuck from across the room, my anger swelling with every drag on my cigarette. I could hardly blink for the rage. I thought I could kill him and feel no remorse.

I switched my focus to Stephen, who had showed up for my "birthday party" like a good daddy, and brought along his bimbo-du-jour. He didn't laugh with the crowd like she did, but he said nothing. He did nothing to help Sara.

I'll never understand that. His affair with Sara destroyed his friendship with Alfie. Stephen and Alfie were best friends since grade school. The affair must have meant something to Stephen. He must have cared about Sara.

Why didn't he do something to help her?

Why didn't he do something to help me?

Satisfied with her performance, Chuck placed a pill on Sara's tongue, and everybody clapped. End scene.

Chuck disappeared soon after. I finished my cigarette and considered my options. I was desperate to get rid of him, and nobody else was going to make that happen. In a mega-mansion full of people that included my mother and my father, I was all alone.

I figured I could use Chuck's attraction to me to score some drugs from him. And then maybe I could finally get him out of the house. After all, someone's got to pay for it when a teenage girl ends up high.

I went upstairs to plan my next move. The faint sound of an acoustic guitar grew louder as I walked down the hall toward my room. I found Chuck there, sitting on my bed and playing my guitar.

I'm not sure what was more infuriating: that he was on my bed or that he was touching my guitar. Jett had given me that guitar. Chuck had no right to touch it. Nobody did. If I hadn't loved the guitar so much, I think I would have grabbed it from him and beat him to death with it.

Chuck smiled when he saw me. I had a fleeting thought that it was nice to see a smile instead of the usual oh-fuck-you're-still-here look I got from Sara, but then I remembered who was doing the smiling and pushed that thought out of my mind.

There was no hint of the unnerved Chuck I'd seduced (gag) earlier in the kitchen. That Chuck had been fresh out of bed and sober, or as sober as he ever got. That Chuck wasn't yet fueled by drugs like this one, and I was all out of whiskey.

He stopped playing the guitar and set it aside, holding out his hand. "Come here."

I stayed put. "You have something for me?"

"I might have," he said.

"Show me."

His smirk stretched on. "How can I when you're way over there?"

I stayed put, eyeing him. He sighed, procuring a bottle of whiskey and a glass from beside him. "Here. Would this help your nerves?"

Greatly, actually!

"I can get that for myself," I said. "Where's the good stuff?"

I was pathetic. I mean, I really was.

He got up and crossed to me, pouring a drink as he did. He handed it to me and then leaned against the wall next to the door, looking me up and down. It made my stomach turn. I drank the alcohol to give my hands something to do other than smack the leer off his face.

He watched me, clearly amused. "You don't like me much, do you?"

How astute.

"I don't really know you," I said.

He tucked a piece of my hair behind my ear. "And whose fault is that?"

I shrugged.

"I want us to be friends," he said. "Do you think we could be friends, Alice?"

He looked down at me, waiting for an answer, so I nodded. He smiled a Cheshire grin.

How appropriate.

Without warning (without warning that I recognized, anyhow), he grabbed the back of my neck and crushed his lips to mine. It was about then I realized I was in over my head.

Abort mission.

I struggled free and shoved him away. "Get off me!"

He fell back, laughing. "Ah, I'm on to you, Little One."

The room shifted suddenly. I teetered and reached out to keep from falling. Unfortunately, the only something within reach was Chuck. He (oh-so-graciously) put his arms around me to hold me up.

"All right, love?" he asked.

From the way he said it, I knew he knew I wasn't all right.

"What did you do?" I asked. My voice was an echo and the room became a vortex. "What did you do to me?"

"Only what you asked," he said. He withdrew a bottle of pills from his pocket and shook it. "The good stuff."

I dropped the glass and pushed away from him, but my coordination and strength plummeted, and he tightened his hold on me. Panic set in at the realization that I was at his mercy.

"Be careful what you wish for, Alice," he whispered.

My legs gave out and I was in his arms, just like in the movies. He carried me to my bed and set me down gently. It would have been romantic if he hadn't just drugged me, and he wasn't my mother's boyfriend.

He tied a rubber band around my upper arm and probed the skin in the crook of my elbow.

"Do you think I'm stupid, Alice?" he said.

Yes.

"What was your plan?" he asked. "Get drugs from me and then tell on me?"

Yes.

He held my face in his hands, managing a pitiful frown. "Are you under the impression anybody would care?"

I was too out of it to realize what he planned. I didn't even see the syringe until he plunged the needle into my arm and pumped its contents into me.

The relief was immediate, Diary. There was more comfort in that rush of heat than I'd felt in my entire life. Any fight that remained in me was gone.

"That's it," said Chuck. His breath was warm in my ear as he stretched out beside me. He cradled my head to his chest. "You need to understand, Alice. If you make her choose between me and you, she'll choose me."

I was vaguely aware of his hands in my hair, his lips against the side of my head, the feel of his fingertips as he stripped away my clothing, but his voice and his movements were far away. Everything seemed so very far away, and warm, and it was as if nothing would ever be wrong again.

Later that night, I woke up alone. The warmth had faded. My lips and thighs were bruised and there weren't enough blankets to vanquish the cold.

I could hear them downstairs. Laughing. Celebrating.

Happy fucking birthday to me.

Fifteen should be too young for the world to break you.

REUNION

The hours that followed were a blur.

To this day, it's bizarre when I think back on it. It's like I'm recalling some other girl's memories, a girl who looks just like me but is completely removed from my reality.

I remember that girl locking herself in my bathroom.

I remember her taking the pills.

I remember her slashing her wrist.

It's me again, though, when I think about the foyer. I woke up, or I should say, came to, on a gurney on the foyer floor, surrounded by paramedics and party-goers. Chuck was cowering in the crowd, looking equal parts guilty and afraid. Stephen was crouching against the wall with his head in his hands. I think he was crying.

So...now he cared?

Beside him, Sara wailed. "I don't understand. I don't know what's going on," she choked through tears, clutching at Jett's jacket. "Why is this happening, Jett?"

The tears were clearly for her, Sara, not for me.

At least "mom" was sticking to the program.

Jett. Beautiful Jett Andrews, with his charming Irish brogue and kind eyes. He loves me to this day as if

I were his own child and pays more attention to me than Stephen ever has.

Jett ignored Sara's pleas but held her to keep her from falling over. His pale face was wet and streaked with crimson. Blood soaked the white shirt beneath his jacket, and his hands were also red. I remember feeling worried...panicked that he'd hurt himself. I remember thinking the EMTs should have been helping him, not fussing over me.

And then I passed out.

However, thanks to the fucking tabloids, I know exactly what happened next, and so does everybody else in the world. Some asshole that was at the party sold his first-hand account to the highest bidder:

It was bad! Jett had carried Alice down the stairs, shouting for someone to call 911. She was covered in blood and so was he.

The paramedics showed up and Jett told them she'd taken a bunch of pills and cut her wrist. They shoved a tube down her throat and she thrashed around a bit, but I think she'd already passed out. The blood soaked right through the gauze they wrapped around her wrist.

They put a big syringe on the end of the tube and pumped some kind of fluid into her. I watched them suction it out, bit by bit, and hoped like hell that never happened to me. It was brutal.

But what happened next was completely insane. Stephen's face was suddenly full of rage. Sara gasped and seemed to lose all strength in her legs. Jett let a bunch of nasty words fly and lowered her to the ground, stepping toward the door at the same time.

I followed their line of sight to see Stuart had just stepped into the foyer, and with him, Alfie Evans.

Fuck. Alfie Evans in Sara's house again. The rest of us gasped when we saw him too.

"What are you doing here?" Stephen growled, leaping to his feet.

"He was with me when Jett called," said Stuart.

Stephen charged at Alfie, grabbing him by his jacket. Stuart wedged himself between them and ripped Stephen away. Stephen lost his footing so Stuart was practically dragging Stephen with him. He tossed Stephen to the floor and stood over him, fists clenched.

"Your daughter's dying, and all you can focus on is him?" said Stuart.

Stephen scrambled to his feet right away. "I don't want him anywhere near her!"

"Which her, mate?" said Alfie.

Alice writhed right then. I swear to God, man, it was like it was his voice that did it, his voice that woke her up. Like a really fucked up version of Sleeping Beauty or something. Or maybe it was because they'd just ripped the tube out.

I heard one of the paramedics ask, "Someone riding in the ambulance with her?" which was pointless because nobody was listening. They were too busy fighting with each other.

The paramedics kind of looked at each other then, and one of them made this curly-Q gesture near her temple, you know, like, "They're all nuts!"

That's about when I came to again. And yes, it was the tube being ripped out of my throat that woke me up. It wasn't Alfie's voice, for Christ's sake—these people and their fucking theories.

It was all very fuzzy. Like a dream. I saw them there: Sara, Alfie, Stuart, and Stephen. Together again, with Jett watching over them.

I put my head back. The statues kept their watch over me as the paramedics wheeled me out of the house.

"Is she—is she laughing?" said one of the paramedics.

"I think she is," said the other.

"What the fuck?" muttered the first.

But, it was funny. It really was.

Diary, don't you see? Fifteen years after tearing them apart, I'd finally gotten the band back together.

IT SHOULD HAVE BEEN YOU

There were so many days back then when I wondered when I'd wake up from the nightmare. Those were the good days. It was the days when I knew for sure that this was my life...those were the bad days.

As penance for trying to off myself, despite my insistence that was not the case, I was shipped off to rehab after I was released from the psych ward at the hospital. I told some counselors there about what had happened to me, but I didn't tell them Chuck was the culprit. Talking about him with strangers wasn't going to help. I really just wanted to forget about the whole thing and move on. Plus, Chuck had a point. I'd gotten exactly what I'd wished for. I just hadn't followed through on my end.

Also, the only person whose opinion about Chuck mattered couldn't have cared less. Want proof? After drugging and raping me on my fifteenth birthday, Chuck was allowed to stay in that house with Sara for several years. No, Sara never knew what he did to me, but she knew something had happened. Kids don't just slice their wrists open for no reason, but she didn't care to investigate. She didn't even visit me at the hospital or at rehab.

To this day, I maintain I did not try to kill myself that night. I don't deny taking the pills or that I cut my wrist, but I deny wanting to die.

Because here's the thing: Not wanting to live and wanting to die are two completely different things. The real problem is lack of options.

My name is Alice. I've been sober for one week.

Hi, Alice.

What a joke.

It took about a week of that bullshit at Second Fucking Chances rehabilitation facility to decide I wanted out. I wanted out of my so-called family, and I wanted it to be legal, so I petitioned the court to become emancipated.

Jett was the only one who objected to it.

"You're only fifteen, Alice," he said.

You're only fifteen.

No shit!

I would've loved to have parents who took care of me. It wasn't asking for a lot, in my opinion. I didn't need for them to actually love me. Giving a tiny shit whether I lived or died would've sufficed.

Jesus Christ.

The emancipation process was much simpler than I thought it would be. In California, to be considered for emancipation, all of the following must be true:

1. You are at least fourteen years old.

Beat it by a year! Check.

2. You do not want to live with your parents.

Yeah. Check.

3. Your parents don't mind if you move out.

Done. Sara was glad I was gone. She'd been waiting for that for fifteen years. Chuck might have testified he'd rather I stayed at the house, but unluckily for him he had no legal right over me.

I wasn't one hundred percent sure what Stephen's reaction would be, but he seemed to be okay with it, and not in the apathetic way Sara was. I overheard Jett talking to him in the hallway outside my room at rehab not long after I filed the paperwork.

"Do you know what emancipation means?" said Jett.

"I know what it means," said Stephen.

"And you're going to let her do it?" said Jett. "You're going to let her move out on her own?"

Stephen hesitated. "It's what she wants, Jett. Who am I to stand in her way?"

Jett released that exasperated noise from his throat that he makes whenever he's aggravated. "You're her father!"

Jett was a calm man. He rarely lost control of his emotions, and I'm not sure how considering he worked with spoiled rock stars day in and day out.

I could almost hear the stubble against the back of his fingers as he brushed his cheek with them, struggling to compose himself.

"She doesn't want to live with me. She's said as much," said Stephen. "What am I supposed to do?"

A silence followed.

"It should've been you, mate," said Stephen, his voice muffled.

I scooted closer to the door and peaked into the hall. Stephen was hunched over on the bench just outside my door, elbows on his knees. Jett stood beside him.

"You should've been her father," continued Stephen. "You're much better at it than I am."

"It's not a matter of being better," said Jett, sitting beside him. "It's a matter of putting her needs before yours."

"That's what I'm trying to do," said Stephen.

Stephen lifted his head and looked at the ceiling. His skin was ashen in the harsh florescent lighting, and he hadn't shaved in days. He hadn't slept in days either judging from the thick bags under his eyes, and he was too thin. He looked awful.

Is it bad that it made me feel good to see him so distraught? Not good. Good isn't the right word. Encouraged, maybe. Hopeful.

"I mean, look what's happened to her," said Stephen. "I don't know how to say this without it sounding like a complete cop out, but she's better off without me."

More silence.

Stephen continued. "Can you honestly tell me you think she's better off with me than on her own?"

Jett couldn't tell him that.

"They'd be stupid to deny her request, frankly," said Stephen. "It's what she deserves. I'm not going to stand in her way."

Jett sighed. "But—"

"I'm not abandoning her," said Stephen. "If she wants me around I will be. But she deserves a shot at a life where her parents aren't constantly fucking it up for her."

Maybe he loved me after all?

Where was I? Oh, yes. Emancipation stipulations.

4. You can handle your own money.

5. You have a legal way of making money.

Uh oh. Roadblock.

I had absolutely no money of my own to speak of, and as the allegedly suicidal, drug-addicted teenage child of rock stars, my prospects for gainful employment were not great.

Enter Jett.

After Jett married Sara, he created a trust in my name and put a percentage of his own earnings into it every month. At the time it was created, the trust was to be signed over to me when I turned twenty-one, but after the emancipation filing, Jett agreed in court to release a monthly allowance to me.

(If you're wondering why Sara married Jett and not the father of her child, the answer is simple: Stephen didn't ask her. Their affair and pregnancy destroyed a lifelong friendship, broke up rock's most beloved couple, and effectively ended the greatest rock band in history, but the idea of settling down was taking it a bit too far.)

The last stipulation?

6. Emancipation would be good for you.

This one sounded pretty subjective to me; good for me from whose perspective? Mine? Absolutely. Chuck's? Definitely not. Sara's? Not applicable. The judge's? Who the fuck knows?

Yeah, that one got a little tricky.

"Due to events in the minor's recent past," I was asked to submit to a mental health evaluation by a court-appointed psychologist. The results of this evaluation would help the judge determine whether or not I was mentally stable enough to handle life on my own.

That was fun.

It's kind of hard to convince a stranger you aren't suicidal when you've got a still-healing, self-inflicted slash across your wrist. My argument that, had I really wanted to die, I would have cut perpendicular to my wrist instead of parallel was not well-received.

Somehow though, after several question-and-answer sessions, the psychologist felt confident enough about my mental state to tell the judge she didn't believe I would leap in front of the nearest bus as soon as I was on my own.

It only helped my case that the parties at Sara's house were legendary. Legends are hearsay, at best, and couldn't be used as evidence in court, but it was hard for anybody to argue that I was better off with either of my parents. The judge ruled in my favor, and I left rehab an officially emancipated minor.

Jett asked me to come live with him once I was out, but I respectfully declined. Jett was still heavy into the music industry. He still managed the members of *Wonderland* in their solo careers, and I didn't begrudge him that. It was his livelihood. But I wanted a fresh start, a clean break, and staying with Jett would not have accomplished that.

So, I (Jett) found a crappy little apartment (crappy only when compared to Sara's mansion) in Santa Monica and helped me move my stuff in. He had it furnished for me so the only items I really had to move in were my clothes and my guitar. It didn't take long.

We nicknamed the apartment...wait for it...Alice's Place.

Creative, yes?

HAPPY NOW?

Not long after the move to Alice's Place, I noticed a sign in the window of a new pub down the street: Coming Soon: Open Mic Night.

The bar name? The Rabbit Hole.

Yes, I'm serious. That's really its name.

"You're Alice Moriarty," said one of the bartenders when I stopped in to inquire about their open mic night.

"No," I said, too quickly. "No, I'm not."

"The Wonderland kid?" asked the other.

"No," I repeated.

"Dude, that's perfect."

So much for anonymity.

A third guy, the owner, as it turned out, winked and leaned in closer, whispering, "Your secret's safe with me."

It wasn't, but I appreciated his effort. They put me on the marquee that week, which seemed to me to defeat the purpose of open mic night, but oh well.

Marquee might be too strong a word, too. It was really just a rusted out, old sign that couldn't keep hold of all the letters they crammed into it. For the longest time, the sign read: Tonight: ALI E MORI TY. The people who showed up called me "Alie Mority" and that was fine with me. Anything but "Little One" or "the Wonderland kid" would do.

I played mostly cover songs, slipping in an original song here and there. Three months in, the place was standing room only. By then, they'd gotten a new sign out front and planted my proper name on it. I didn't know (and still don't) if so many people showed up to see me because of who my parents were or because they genuinely enjoyed listening to me play. It was nice, whatever the reason.

About six months into my tenure at The Rabbit Hole (or "The Hole" as it was more charmingly known), a man who looked an awful lot like Alfie Evans walked in the door. He wore a baseball cap crammed low on his forehead and kept to himself at the back. He didn't order a drink. He didn't talk to anybody, and nobody made a fuss about him. He just watched me play a few songs and then left. I'd only ever seen him twice in person, and, admittedly, the second time was under fairly strenuous circumstances, but I knew it was him. What I didn't know was why the hell he was there.

Remember the first time I ever saw him?

They say you never forget your first time.

I was wearing those ridiculous purple footie pajamas Jett got me for Christmas that year, the first time I ever saw Alfie in person.

I was wandering the house, discreetly checking out the party situation when the doorbell rang. I scooted through the foyer and up the stairs out of sight, since I was supposed to be in bed.

Random Fucking Party Guy answered the door. The man at the door asked for Jett. Jett had moved out just that week but Party Guy was not in the know, because he wandered off in search of him, leaving the visitor alone at the door.

That was when I caught my very first look at Alfie Evans in the flesh. That messy black hair and those tortured black eyes.

This was the man on my album cover.

✓ *You've got blue eyes like him, Little One.* ✓

A year after Alfie left *Wonderland* he released a solo album called *Little One*. The first single he released, the album's title track, is clearly about a child, a child he called "Little One." Because of the way (and the reason) Alfie left *Wonderland*, everybody in the world assumed the song was about me, so for as long as I can remember "Little One" has been my nickname.

Making matters worse, Alfie has never confirmed or denied this assumption, so over time the legend has grown to ridiculous heights. Some fans have even theorized he is my biological father.

It's annoying. The song. The nickname. All of it.

Actually, that's not entirely true. The song is pretty great. Think "Hey Jude" meets *The Cure*. It's almost sweet; brooding, but sweet, and that's why I'm not so sure it's about me.

By all accounts, Alfie has hated me since the day I was born, since before I was born, really, for ruining what he had with Sara. Her affair with Stephen was too much for him to forgive. Certainly, the child resulting from that affair would be mortal enemy number one. Why, then, would he write such a nice song about me?

Why, Alfie?

How special could his relationship have been with Sara, though, if she was banging Stephen on the side? How close could Stephen and Alfie have been? It's not like I was the product of a drunken, one-night stand. I was the product of a drunken, months-long affair.

Fucking rock stars.

Along with those footie pajamas that Christmas, Jett gave me a copy of the *Little One* album. He played the song for me and said it was about me. I liked it. I liked the pretty man on the cover, and there he was standing in the doorway of my house.

I skipped off to my room to get the album from its place under my mattress. I wanted to show the album to Alfie. I don't know why. I was five. Why the hell does a five year old do anything? Your guess is as good as mine.

When I got back to the stairs, Alfie and Sara were talking quietly. Their voices rose with each step I took down the stairs. By the time I got to the bottom, they were shouting at each other, and he was making a beeline for the door. In the time it took for me to cross the foyer, she was asking him to stay. She held out her hand, and he took it after a long hesitation. Onlookers had gathered at the entry of the Great Room to watch the show.

That's when Alfie spotted me.

Little chump me holding up his album, grinning like a goddamn idiot.

Hi there! I'm the thing that ruined your life. Nice to meet you! I really like your album!

I even grabbed one of his fingers, for fuck's sake.

It embarrasses me to this day. I'll be going along, minding my own business, and a memory of it will pop into my head. I'll lose my breath a moment and my face will flush. It sucks.

That night, Alfie jerked his finger away from me so hard he almost fell over.

Abandon ship!

"You're supposed to be in bed!" shouted Sara.

"I never should have come here," said Alfie, stepping back.

He tripped over himself to get to the door. Sara grabbed at him, but he shoved her hands away. As the door slammed behind him, she threw herself at it.

"Come back!" she said, pounding the door with her open hand. "Please come back."

She peeled herself from the door and hurled her glass at it. I clamped my hands over my ears as it shattered, and she collapsed onto her haunches, putting her face in her hands.

When she pulled herself to her feet, she turned to me. "Happy now?" she asked, her voice low.

I didn't answer her. What the hell would I have said? "Yeah, ma. I'm great?"

She stumbled up the stairs. I shoved my way through a sea of partiers to the fireplace in the Great Room and threw the album in the fire.

"Yeah! Burn it up, Little One!" said Chuck.

He was sitting at the corner of the stoop of the fireplace cutting cocaine with a razor blade. He arranged some of the powder in a neat row on the glass and put his nose to it. A quick sniff and the line disappeared up his nostril, just like in the movies. Some kids learned about life by watching movies. I learned about what was in the movies by watching my life.

Chuck watched me watching him and then stood, holding out the mirror. "Want some?"

Stuart stepped between us and slapped the mirror from Chuck's hands, scooping me into his arms. The mirror broke on the floor and the cocaine cascaded off of it, leaving a tiny plume in its wake.

"She's only five," said Stuart through clenched teeth.

"Looks like she could use it too," said Chuck, unconcerned about his fallen drug and paraphernalia. He surely had more nearby. "Two minutes with Evans will do that to anybody."

A few people chuckled. Stuart didn't. He shielded me with his body and stared Chuck down until he moved away.

"Come on," said Stuart. "Let's get you back up to bed."

Stuart took me back upstairs to my bedroom and tucked me in.

Come to think of it, I think that was the first night I met Chuck, too.

LUCKY

Life from sixteen to twenty was pretty good and not just in comparison to the first fifteen. My open mic residency at The Hole morphed into a regular, paid gig. I was paid ten percent of total cover charges plus tips. By the time I was eighteen, I stopped dipping into the Trust of Jett and started cranking out a nice little living for myself. Alice's Place became a home. It was the first time I really felt at home somewhere.

I visited Stephen and stayed at his house from time to time, mostly to keep him company during his droughts between girlfriends, but I didn't see or speak to Sara for over five years. I wouldn't have seen her at all if it hadn't been for the *Wonderland* reunion tour.

Yeah. Can you believe it? *Wonderland* was getting back together, and not in the everybody-gather-round-because-Alice-just-sliced-and-diced-herself way like last time.

Rumors of a reunion had surrounded the members of the band pretty much since the day they broke up, but the rumors never panned out. I think they'd tried from time to time, but their egos wouldn't allow for anything concrete to develop. Sara's and Alfie's egos, that is.

This is a sample of how I imagine those attempts went:

Sara: "Why don't we do this song instead?"

Alfie: "Because you fucked my best friend."

Of course they wouldn't have been in the same room together, so it would have been Jett relaying the messages back and forth, like an intermediary on a grade school playground.

But, earlier this year, the members of *Wonderland* somehow put their differences aside and negotiated successfully, and a full reunion world tour was booked before anybody changed their minds. Tickets went on sale within weeks, and every show—seventy-two in total—sold out in a matter of minutes.

It seemed unfathomable to me that they would attempt a reunion tour, especially one on such a grand scale. By all accounts, Sara's mental and physical health had deteriorated since the last time I'd seen her, and that was saying something. I couldn't understand how they thought she could make it through seventy-two shows, and with Alfie, no less. The stress alone would envelope her.

But, there was hope...

It was about a week before they went into rehearsals, at the beginning of July, when Jett told me Chuck was finally gone. He hadn't left the house willingly or quietly, but he had left nonetheless. Sara told Jett she wanted Chuck gone, and Jett had taken care of it. He'd dragged Chuck out the front door, through the security gate and literally threw him out into the street.

I wish I'd been there to see it.

I also wish I hadn't gone to see Sara after Jett told me the news. I should have known better. (I Should

Have Known Better will be etched on my gravestone someday.) I should have just trusted what Jett said, and let it be, but I wanted to see for myself that Chuck was really gone.

Her alarm codes were the same and my key still worked in the front door, so I let myself into the house and found Sara curled up in her giant bed, lost in a sea of blankets. She was writing in her journal.

I watched her for a while before alerting her to my arrival. I could see her cheekbones from the doorway and the hollows beneath them. She'd lost another ten pounds from a body that desperately needed to gain twenty. Her pill bottles were lined up like soldiers on her nightstand.

I thought I should greet her with something poignant. This was a reunion, after all. Five years in the making. I took in a breath, opening my mouth to speak.

Cue the dramatic music.

"Hi," I said.

She looked up and greeted me with that same old look of surprise.

"What are you doing here?" she said.

Right. No time for small talk.

"Jett told you the news?" said Sara, examining me.

"It's true then?" I said. "He's gone?"

"Your spy wouldn't lie to you, Alice."

Her bitterness hadn't changed much.

I stepped into the room and walked to the bed.

"How many of these do you take a day?" I asked, reading the label on one of the pill bottles.

Sara snatched it from me but not before I caught a glimpse of the dosage. It was no wonder she was such a fucking zombie all the time. It certainly didn't seem like much had changed since I'd been there last. And how could it have? The prescribed dosage of that particular drug could've KO'd a horse, and it was only one of five or six bottles.

"Jesus," I said.

"What?"

"You're going to try and make it through a tour taking all these pills?" I said.

"What do you care?" she asked.

"You're my mother," I said.

She laughed. "Since when?"

Have you ever heard that quote, "when someone shows you who they are, believe them"? I think it was Maya Angelou who said it. That came to mind then. It's good advice. I wonder when I'll learn to fucking heed it.

"Have a nice life, Sara," I muttered, turning to leave.

"You left me," she said.

Thinking I must have heard her wrong, I turned back to her. "What?"

"You left me," she said.

"I left you?"

"You left me just like all the rest of them," she said.

I could have spit it at her.

"All the rest of them..." I repeated, nodding. Tension slinked like a snake from my jaw down my neck and into my shoulders. "So you're comparing me to—to, who? Alfie?"

It was the first time I'd ever said his name in her presence. It actually might've been the first time I ever said his name out loud.

Sara sprang up like a spooked cat. "Don't talk about him."

"That's who you mean, right?" I asked. Rage clambered up my throat. "I left just like Alfie left?"

"Stop," she said.

"I abandoned you just like he abandoned you?"

"Stop it," she said.

"You abandoned me!" I shouted.

"That's not true," she said.

"You chose your drugs and your men over me, and you have the balls to say I abandoned you?"

"Stop saying that," she said.

"Come on, Sara! It's just us here," I said. "There's no reason to lie. Just admit it."

She refused.

Her pills beckoned me. I charged over to the nightstand again and scooped them up.

Sara forced herself out of bed and blocked my path to the door. She eyed the pills and then me, and then the pills again, like a mother whose children were about to be kidnapped. Well, like a mother who would give a damn if her kids were about to be kidnapped. I've heard those mothers exist.

"Give those back," said Sara.

"Choose, Sara," I said. "Me or the pills?"

"Give them back."

"Me or the pills?"

She lunged for them, but it was a clumsy attempt, and I dodged her easily, sprinting into the hall. She followed. I held the pills over my head out of her reach, and it reminded me of that night, when Chuck did the same thing to her.

She jumped, over and over, clawing at the bottles.

"Look at you!" I said, laughing. "You're pathetic!"

Admittedly, it wasn't my finest moment.

"I wouldn't be this way if it wasn't for you!" screamed Sara.

To be fair, in that moment, I probably deserved that.

But still. Damn.

She gave up the jumping and pushed me.

A strong breeze would have knocked her over, but the force of that shove was inhuman. I fell into the railing above the foyer, trying to regain my footing on the hardwood floors. I was too stunned by the first attack to evade the second.

"You're lucky your father wanted you!"

She shoved me again.

I flipped over the railing.

The pill bottles came loose from my hand. They hit the foyer floor and broke open a split second before my body did the same.

It was all too familiar. The paramedics. Sara's wails. That fucking floor. It'd been over five years since I'd last seen her, and it took me less than five minutes to regret the decision to see her again.

The fall broke my arm, two of my ribs, and fractured one of my vertebrae. I hit my head, too, and was put in a medically induced coma for several days while the swelling in my brain subsided.

After I was released, I was prescribed a bunch of pills for the injuries. Painkillers I'd been advised not to take because of my "previous addiction" to substances.

Sara didn't visit me once during those weeks I was in the hospital.

After all, there was a tour to rehearse for.

Sara Adams was dead to me.

BE CAREFUL WHAT YOU WISH FOR
(TAKE TWO)

It's been about five months since that day.

It took me three months to recover enough to play at The Hole again. My regulars greeted me with a "Welcome Back" cake my first night back, and *Wonderland* kicked off their reunion tour about a week later.

Last night, I took a detour on my way to The Hole and stopped at the Hollywood Bowl scenic overlook.

The overlook is a pretty big tourist trap on Mulholland that has an iconic, panoramic view of downtown Los Angeles, the Hollywood sign and the Pacific on a clear day. There's room for a handful of cars in the parking lot, but the lot is often overrun with those "see the stars's homes" tourist vans, so sightseers's cars are often crammed into the side of the snaking street.

Sara's house is on the list for many of those tours. All of them, I would bet. Her house isn't far from the overlook.

As the name suggests, the spot also overlooks the Hollywood Bowl amphitheatre. *Wonderland* had been on the road for about a couple months. They arrived home to Los Angeles this week to play a series of shows at the Hollywood Bowl, the first of which was last night.

The overlook was a place I could go and check out the show without actually being at it. The last thing I wanted was to be photographed in the audience.

I stood on a patch of dirt just off the designated tourist path and looked down at the open amphitheatre. It's not a close view, but I could see the lights and see and hear the crowd. I could hear the thump of Stuart's bass drum and the rumble of Stephen's bass guitar. Alfie's and Sara's voices mixed with his guitar and drifted up to me over the Hollywood Hills.

I left when the whispering began, ignoring the side-eye stares of the tourists as I made my way down the concrete steps to my car. A couple of them took my picture, but it was nearly dusk, and the light was terrible, so I didn't mind. They weren't going to get any good shots.

Later, my sell-out crowd at The Hole shouted for me to play a *Wonderland* song as I finished my set. They always do. I never oblige. Last night was no different.

"Aww, come on!" shouted one. "We came to see you tonight instead of them."

"That's because you're all broke and pathetic," I said, and they laughed. "Maybe next time."

"You always say that," said another.

"And you keep coming back," I said. "Why would I jinx myself now?"

A waitress handed me a shot and pointed to the man who'd bought it for me. I held it up to him to show my appreciation but didn't drink it, carrying it with me to my tiny room beside the stage.

I set the shot on the counter and stared at it. I stuck my finger in it, touched it to my lips and then licked them.

But I dumped it in the trash before I went any further and then flopped down onto a worn love seat against the wall. I put my head back and closed my eyes, listening to the drone of voices from the front room. A small television played in the corner.

I was close to dozing off when a familiar voice came into earshot from the TV. It was the narrator from one of those music documentary shows that were all the rage in the 90s, when they still played music on music television.

"...despite its very public breakup over two decades ago, *Wonderland* remains one of the best selling bands of all time."

I groaned and opened my eyes, rolling my head toward the TV. Now that *Wonderland* was back on tour, they were everywhere again.

"We asked its members, in separate interviews, about the fateful night it all came to a shocking end," said the narrator.

Sara appeared on screen first. The documentary had been shot after the last time I saw her. She looked a bit healthier; tired still, but healthier. She'd gained some weight. Her face was pale but not so gaunt.

"I tripped as we came off-stage, down the stairs. Alfie caught me, surprisingly. We were in such a bad place at the time, I would have let him fall and kicked him while he was down," she said, laughing. Her laugh faded quickly. "He broke my fall and got up first. That was that."

Next up was Stephen. He'd been drinking. He wasn't drunk yet, but he'd definitely been drinking.

Nobody else might have noticed, not even the interviewer sitting across from him, but I could see it in his eyes—the slight paranoia behind the blue. Stephen thought the worst of people when he drank.

"Alfie hadn't known about the pregnancy yet. Nobody had but us, me and Sara. I came off stage and saw her on the ground, saw him standing over her like that... I just lost it."

Sara again. "It wasn't a stretch for him to think that. The drugs, the booze. Alfie and I went after each other a lot in those days."

Stuart came next. "It was absolute madness. I'd never seen him so angry. Stephen had always been the calmest one of the bunch."

Finally, Alfie appeared. The years had been kind. He looked younger than the other two men even though all three were approaching their mid-50s. He made little eye contact with the interviewer or the camera, choosing instead to focus mostly on the floor.

I sat up and grabbed a smoke.

"He attacked me. My best friend. It shocked the hell out of me," said Alfie, pausing to drag from his cigarette. "Nobody even knew about their affair."

Over a montage of photos and videos of *Wonderland*, way back when, in happier times (pre-Alice), the narrator spoke again. "That night marked the end for *Wonderland*, as well as for rock's reining couple. Evans disappeared from the public eye, emerging a year later as a successful solo artist, as did Adams, who gave birth later that year to a healthy baby girl. In true *Wonderland* style, she and Stephen named their daughter Alice."

"Ugh," I groaned, slapping both hands over my face. So fucking cheesy.

"Rumors of a reunion have surrounded Wonderland for decades. Now, it's finally happening," said the narrator.

"Have you forgiven him?" asked the interviewer of Alfie.

"Who?" said Alfie.

"Stephen."

"Forgiven him for what?"

"For that night," said the interviewer.

Alfie began to fidget, tucking his arms to his chest. He shrugged. "We were all out of our minds back then."

The interviewer pressed him. "What about for the affair? And Sara? Have you forgiven her?"

Alfie dropped his head and cast a resentful glance up at the interviewer.

The screen changed back to Sara then. The editors of the documentary really knew how to maximize the emotional manipulation of its audience.

"The first meeting was good," said Sara. "If Alfie and I can get through rehearsals without killing each other, this might just work."

Stephen was next, of course. "We're older now. Wiser, allegedly. So much was left on the table back then. We've got a lot left to accomplish as a band, I think."

Stuart rolled his eyes. "Christ. Who knows with his bunch?"

Back to Alfie. "I think it's going to be a fucking disaster."

I laughed at that one. I couldn't help it. Don't tell anyone.

Sara appeared again, and she was riled up. "Of course he thinks it's going to be a disaster! He can't let anything go. Never could." She sat back and lit a cigarette, tossing the lighter aside. She exhaled the smoke roughly and folded her arms, looking away from the camera. "He's never forgiven me, in all these years. A huge part of that man will always be stuck in the past."

Alfie chuckled, scratching a spot on his forehead with his cigarette-wielding hand, shaking his head. "And that woman (he emphasized "that woman") will forever believe she knows what I'm feeling."

They then showed a snippet of the *Little One* video. Alfie looked ridiculous with choppy eighties hair and thick eyeliner. Stuart played drums on the track and appeared in the video.

"What about Alice?" asked the interviewer.

The screen changed to Alfie, who looked momentarily bewildered. That shit drives me crazy. You'd think after twenty fucking years somebody would have been used to being asked about me. Christ, whenever any of them were asked anything about me it was always like, "uhh, Alice?"

"Alice?" asked Alfie.

See?

"What about her?" he asked.

"You tell me," said the interviewer.

Alfie stared at the floor, considering. He whispered my name, almost as a spoken thought, and then spoke a bit louder. "I don't know Alice. We've never met."

Pfft.

The camera stayed on him, drawing slowly closer.

"Never?" said the interviewer skeptically.

Alfie looked briefly into the camera. It was as if our eyes met for a moment.

Here's looking at you, kid.

He returned his eyes to the interviewer. "Never."

I jumped up and clicked off the TV. "Liar."

I was bombarded by paparazzi as I walked out of The Hole. It's not uncommon for me to spot them hovering nearby when I go out in public. The unwanted love child of rock stars was a big money-maker for those guys. But, for the most part, they took their pictures quietly and left me alone.

Last night was different. Last night there seemed to be hundreds of them, and they were rabid.

At first, I didn't think too much of it. *Wonderland* was in town. Interest in them was at an all-time high. I thought maybe they just wanted a sound byte about them or something.

But they swarmed me as I tried to walk to my car, blinding me with their flashes. They shouted question after question at me.

"Do you know what happened?"

"How is she?"

"Are you on the way to the hospital?"

That last question gave me reason to slow my progression.

"The hospital?" I asked.

"Are you on your way there now?"

"What is her prognosis?"

"Can you tell us what happened?"

I pulled up and turned to them. "What the hell are you talking about?"

A silence washed over them. The flashes continued.

Finally, one of them answered. "You haven't heard?"

Once they realized I had no idea what they were talking about, they clued me in that something had happened to Sara. Something bad. They said an ambulance had been called to the amphitheatre after the show, and that Sara had been taken out on a stretcher and rushed to the hospital.

I asked if they knew which hospital she'd been taken to. They didn't, but they made some phone calls and had the information pretty quickly. Sometimes, those guys are handy to have around.

One of them drove me to the hospital. There were too many of them to find my car, and I was too freaked out to drive anyhow. I think I agreed to an exclusive with him on the way. I have no idea what I said. That should be an interesting article.

I found them in a private waiting room, Stephen and Jett. Stephen was still in his stage clothes. Jett was in his usual I'm-too-fucking-old-to-be-babysitting-rock-stars-still state, but he looked frazzled even for him.

"I called your phone," snapped Jett when he saw me. "Why didn't you answer?"

"I was at the club."

"What good is it you having that thing if you're not going to answer it?" said Jett.

"Someone going to tell me what's going on?"

"Jett found her in her dressing room after the show," said Stephen. "That's all we know so far."

"Found her?" I said. "What do you mean found her?"

Jett opened his mouth to respond, but a voice called out from behind us.

"Mama's been up to her old tricks again."

I turned.

Alfie.

Drunk, pissed-off Alfie.

Of course.

I hadn't noticed him or Stuart when I walked in. They sat together on a couch against the wall. Alfie sat forward with his elbows on his knees, glaring at me with eyes rimmed in smudged black. Stuart was slouched beside him with one of his long legs flung over the arm. They were still in their stage clothes, too.

I wasn't exactly sure what Alfie meant by that. She was up to what old tricks? Sara had lots of tricks, and they weren't all old. The drugs? The men? I was about to ask him when Stuart intervened.

"Idiot," muttered Stuart.

"Fuck off," said Alfie.

"Shut up," said Jett to Alfie. "Alice, ignore him."

"Was it the pills?" I asked, turning back to Jett.

Jett shrugged, sweeping his hair across his forehead with a shaking hand. "I don't know."

"Well, did she fall? Hit her head?" I asked. "Was she bleeding?"

"She wasn't bleeding," said Jett, clearing his throat. He was close to tears.

A doctor appeared then. From the way the men reacted, I gathered he was the doctor who was taking care of Sara. The poor guy looked exhausted, shaken, and very, very sad.

That's always a good sign, right?

"Alice?" he asked.

I nodded. "How is she?"

"We did—we did everything we could," he stammered. "I'm so sorry. She's gone."

Be careful what you wish for, Alice.

THE END OF THE BEGINNING
—December 13, 2009

It's everywhere. Everywhere I look.

"Rock star Sara Adams dead at 50."

Date of death: December 6, 2009.

I decided to start this story, my story, the night she died. I felt it was important to document what was happening.

To do it right, I had to start from the beginning, and fuck, it's been tough getting it all down. I haven't thought about a lot of this stuff in a while, not consciously anyhow. Her death has burrowed a path from my subconscious to my conscious, and I can already feel the weight of it all again.

Her memorial service was yesterday. I didn't go. I couldn't. They think I just don't care that she's dead. I know they do. I can see it in their eyes, but it's not that I don't care. The world has lost an icon. I'm sad for her fans. I'm sad the world has lost Sara Adams, but I lost my mother a long time ago. Attending a memorial service for her now seemed kind of pointless.

Stephen, Stuart, and Jett attended. From the media coverage, it looked to have been a star-studded event, with everybody who was anybody in attendance.

Photographers swarmed the area but were kept out of the gates of the cemetery by security.

Another glaring no-show? Alfie. The Internet has had a ball with that one, speculating why neither of us showed up. One of the more vulgar headlines speculated that Sara had revealed to him on her death bed that he was indeed my biological father, and Alfie and I were off together coming to terms with that shocker. Another suggested he and I had found solace with each other in this dark time. Sexually. Both theories are equally disgusting to me.

Toxicology results aren't in yet, but initial autopsy results revealed cardiac arrest as the cause of death. Well, duh. Isn't that why everybody ultimately dies, because their fucking heart stops beating?

Her fans are distraught. The makeshift memorial they've created at the front gate of her house stretches as long and as high as the gate itself: hand-written cards, teddy bears, flowers. I've read some of the cards. Sara was their best friend, their mentor, even their mother. They're completely lost without her. It makes me kind of mad, too, for them, that she was so irresponsible with her life.

I stopped by Stephen's house last night after the service. We had plans to have dinner together, but he was passed out on the couch when I arrived, hand still clutching his glass. Plans with Stephen are always tentative, at best.

I sat and watched him "sleep" and wondered for the millionth time what my life would have been if he, instead of Sara, had raised me. Raised is probably too strong a word here, but you understand what I mean. Would I despise him now and consider Sara the friend?

Stephen has many faults, but for some reason, I've never resented him like I have Sara.

Was that an oedipal thing? Did I accept Stephen's faults easier than I did Sara's just because he's the opposite sex parent? Is there some sort of dirty psychosis bumping around my subconscious that allows me to forgive him more easily than her? It's not fair to her, really. I should resent them equally. But, mostly, I just want to protect Stephen from himself.

I pried his hand off the glass and pulled a blanket over him, making sure he was on his side.

I washed the dishes in the kitchen and found a pizza in the freezer, shoving it in the oven. I set the timer on the stove and went out to the patio to play my guitar.

I spent some time tuning the guitar and then lit a cigarette, but a hand appeared over my head and plucked the cigarette from my mouth.

"That's a disgusting habit," said Jett, settling into the chair across from me.

"Lurking this evening, are we?" I said, glowering.

"I just got here, actually," said Jett. "How are you doing?"

"I'm fine," I said.

"Fine, fine or stop-asking-me-how-I'm-doing fine?" he said.

I gave him a look.

He smiled. After a few moments, he held out his hands, palms up.

I looked at them, fighting a smile. "No."

"Chicken?" he said.

I narrowed my eyes and feigned disinterest, then tried to slap his hands. He pulled them away at the last second.

"Dammit! Don't," I warned. "Don't do it."

He made an "O" with his thumb and forefinger and put it to his eye. "Too slow, Cheerio."

I laughed. "I forget how fucking corny you can be."

Jett has done the "Too slow, Cheerio" bit for as long as I can remember. He does it whenever he feels I need cheering up. I pretend like I don't like it, that it's annoying, but I pretty much love it.

"It's worth it to see you smile," he said.

Whoops. He slipped. This was a rare occurrence for Jett. He'd made me aware that I was experiencing some joy. Unacceptable for a brooding, basket case like me.

My smile faded. I grabbed my cigarettes.

He sighed. "You can't go a minute without one of those things?"

I lit the stick and dragged on it. "You know, your objections would be easier to stomach if you hid your hypocrisy better."

His eyes narrowed. "What?"

I pointed to the obvious outline of a pack of cigarettes in his front jeans pocket. He grumbled and pulled his suit coat tighter around him, shielding it.

I smiled. "So, to what do I owe the pleasure?"

"I could ask the same of you."

"I'm here for dinner with my father," I said. "In theory."

He nodded. "I've got a band meeting."

"Ah, well, you'd better toss Stephen in the shower and pump him full of coffee if you want him coherent any time soon," I said, mimicking drinking from a bottle.

Jett sighed. "Christ."

"He started in on his dinner a bit early," I said.

"Does that mean you haven't eaten?"

"I'm not a kid anymore," I said. "I found some food all on my own."

"Chinese?"

"Pizza," I said. "It's in the oven now."

"Ah, of course," he said. "And you'll always be a kid to me."

"That's sweet and only a little bit creepy."

"Ha ha," he said.

He tipped his head back and rolled his neck from side to side, eyes closed. His skin seemed almost luminescent in the moonlight. It really brought out the deep circles under his eyes.

"You look tired, Jett."

He nodded, looking back at me. "It's been...difficult. That fucking funeral was like the goddamn Academy Awards. Everyone dressed up in their finest, gagging for the perfect photo op. Never mind the dead lady, everybody!"

When Jett is upset, his Dublin accent is accentuated, as if he mindfully dials it back when he's in normal conversation. I hate to see him upset, but I love the sound of it when he is because every sentence is like poetry. When I was a kid, it was hard for me not to smile when he hollered at me. It still is. It's one of the many things that drive poor Jett insane on a daily basis.

I passed him my smokes and lighter. He snatched them from me and lit one with a grumble, dragging on it before he continued.

"And it goes without saying that there's never a good time for a musician to drop dead, but right in the middle of a highly-promoted, sold-out, world tour is not optimum. She wasn't dead twelve hours before the promoters were crawling up my ass." He threw up air quotes. "'To avoid substantial legal ramifications, it is in the best interest of your clients that we come to a mutually-beneficial solution to this problem.'"

"Christ," I said, cringing.

He nodded, dragging the smoke again. He palpated the skin between his eyes with his thumb. "They could be sued. The band could be sued if we can't figure something out."

"What's there to figure out?" I said. "They can't tour without her."

Jett's head popped up. He studied me a moment.

"What?" I asked.

He blinked, and then blinked again, a sure sign he was about to lie. "Nothing."

"Something," I said.

He blinked again, waving his hand. "No, no. It's nothing. I'm just tired. Fuck, I'm tired."

The stove timer dinged.

"My dinner's ready," I said.

"Allow me," said Jett, standing. "I need to rouse your father anyhow." He hesitated. "Oh, you might want to stay out here for a few minutes."

"I shouldn't come in and say hi to Alfie?" I said, contouring my expression into one of sheer innocence. "Maybe he'd like a slice of my pizza."

Jett gave me the look. I smiled and shooed him away.

I waited what I felt was an appropriate amount of time to allow Alfie to arrive and get downstairs, where their band meetings were held, and then went inside to eat. Jett had the pizza out of the oven and waiting for me.

I made it through half the pizza and then wrapped the rest in plastic wrap. I thought a moment and then grabbed a marker, scrawling "Eat Me" on the plastic wrap. I threw it in the fridge with a smile.

On my way out of the house, I ran into Stuart. Literally. He swept in as I walked out.

"Whoa, sorry!" I said. "I thought you were all downstairs already."

He wrapped me in a bear hug and lifted me off my feet, swinging me around. "You know me and early morning meetings."

"It's eight o'clock at night."

Stuart shrugged. "Everybody down there?"

"I assume so," I said. "I didn't greet everybody personally, of course."

"Lest you be struck down by the glare of the dark prince, you mean?"

I grumbled, and Stuart headed for the basement.

I should have kept going out the front door then. I really should have. I shouldn't have waited a few seconds and then crept down the steps behind Stuart. I should be smarter than that by now, but I think we've already established I'm not.

"Good morning, beautiful," said Jett to Stuart.

Stuart shuffled to the couch and flopped down on it, displacing a grumbling Alfie.

"Now that we can begin, I'll get right to it," said Jett. "I got the call this morning. You're in."

"Hall of Fame?" said Stephen.

Jett nodded.

"Wonderful timing," said Stuart.

"I've been assured the voting took place weeks ago and that this is not, in any way, a shameless exploitation ploy."

Alfie grunted (like a caveman).

Jett continued. "They've asked if you'd perform a tribute to Sara at the ceremony and perform as inductees—two birds, one stone kind of a thing. That leaves us in a bit of a predicament."

"Tell them to fuck off," said Stuart.

Jett sighed. "Brilliant, thank you."

"We've been eligible for, what, seven, eight years? And now suddenly they decide we're worthy?" said Stephen. "Not exploitation, my ass."

"Seems kind of wrong without Sara," said Stuart.

"Sara will be inducted with you," said Jett, clearing his throat. "Posthumously."

What a bummer of a word.

The guys glanced at each other then. They looked a bit shell-shocked still, like maybe Sara would walk down the steps any moment. (Her ghost was probably on the steps trying to trample me.) Alfie looked more tortured than ever. I almost felt bad for him.

Almost.

Jett picked up on that too. "You're awfully quiet over there."

"Just waiting for the other shoe," said Alfie.

"There's an other shoe?" said Stuart.

"There's always an other shoe with him," said Alfie.

Jett hesitated. "I do have an idea."

"There it is," said Alfie.

Jett continued, unrepentant. "Alice."

I almost answered him because I thought he was calling on me.

"Alice?" said Stephen.

Jett nodded. "I want her to perform with you at the ceremony."

What?

"What?" said Alfie, stopping mid-stride.

Out of my head, Evans!

There was an ensuing silence; the kind of silence that's deafening.

Stuart sat up and scratched his head like he was shampooing his hair. "It's not the worst idea I've ever heard."

"It's a horrible idea," said Alfie.

"Why? She's a musician, isn't she?" said Stuart. "A damn fine one, not that you'd know it."

Stephen stood and paced, considering. "The fans?"

"The fans would see it as a touching tribute to her mother," said Jett. He cleared his throat again. "Hopefully."

Alfie snorted. "A touching tribute? I thought they couldn't stand each other?"

"What do you know about it?" said Stephen.

"Not much, as you're all so quick to point out."

"Then shut it," said Stephen.

"Would she do it, though?" said Stuart. "I gather this band hasn't always been her favorite thing in the world."

Ya think?

"I can't believe we're discussing this," said Alfie.

"We're discussing," said Stuart. "You're whining."

The men of *Wonderland* have known each other since grade school. They formed their first band when they were twelve years old and moved to the US together at seventeen. Now, at this point in their lives, the three of them are like an old, married couple.

Also, have I mentioned how much I love Stuart?

Alfie snapped. "We are not doing this!"

Stephen stepped to him. "It's not just your decision to make, is it?"

"Neither of you even wanted that fucking kid!" spat Alfie.

Well. I mean, it's hard to argue his point, but still.

Fuck that guy.

Stephen jumped at Alfie and shoved him against the wall. Frames fell off the wall and books fell off the shelf. They wrestled each other until Stuart and Jett could pry them apart.

"Some things never change," said Alfie.

"You don't talk about Alice."

"Hit a nerve, have I?" said Alfie.

"Keep her name out of your mouth," said Stephen.

Damn. Go Dad!

Actually, it was nothing more than the usual pissing contest between those two. Stephen's anger had less to do with what Alfie said and much more to do with the fact that it was Alfie who'd said it.

Struggling to catch his breath, Stephen doubled over and grasped his side. Alfie leaned against the bookshelf and did the same.

"Fuck, I'm getting too old for this," muttered Stephen.

Alfie grumbled his agreement.

It was silent for a few seconds.

"How am I supposed to not talk about her if she joins the fucking band, mate?" said Alfie, finally.

"We're only talking about one night," said Jett.

"Bullshit!" said Alfie, his energy returning. He turned to Jett. "You forget sometimes how long we've known you, Jett. You're scheming right now. What are we really talking about here?"

Jett sighed and sat. He bowed his head and thumbed the skin between his eyes again. "You're fucked," he admitted.

The other three men exchanged glances and then looked back to Jett.

"I'll assume from your dour expression you don't mean that in the good way," said Stuart.

"The promoters don't want to cancel this tour," said Jett. "I won't bore you with the details but, basically, given the likely nature of Sara's death, their insurers are threatening not to payout."

"Why's that our problem?" said Stuart.

"It shouldn't be," said Jett. "But if the tour is cancelled because you guys refuse to continue on, and their insurers won't cover their losses, the promoters will sue you to get their money back."

Silence.

"Our front woman is dead," said Alfie.

"And the three of you remain," said Jett. "Alfie's a singer. They see no reason why you can't finish the tour."

"Don't we have our own insurance to cover us for this sort of thing?" asked Alfie.

Jett nodded. "Yes, but it's the same thing. They're threatening not to pay. If the promoters sue you and win, and I've consulted some attorney friends who say they are likely to win, that money will come out of your pockets. With the amount of money we're talking about here, it'll likely bankrupt you."

Stephen sat. "Christ."

Alfie finally sat too. He clasped his hands together over his knees and bowed his head.

Silence.

"How many of us have to die for this to all go away?" asked Stuart.

"Stuart," said Jett.

"No, I'm curious. I just wonder what an acceptable amount of death is for these people. Fifty percent? Seventy-five percent? If these two kick off, will I still be expected to bang on my drums by myself for three hours a night?"

I shifted on the step and considered what Jett said. I didn't know the exact numbers without doing some math, but it was likely well into the hundreds of millions of dollars. Jett was right. That would bankrupt them.

"So that's your plan, then?" said Alfie. "Let the world see Alice with us at the Hall of Fame, to soften the blow when we announce we're resuming the tour with her in Sara's place?"

Jett shrugged. "It's an option."

"Jesus Christ," muttered Alfie.

"It's a better option than bankruptcy," said Stuart.

"I'm not so sure," said Alfie.

"Easy for you to say," said Stuart. "You make all the fucking money, don't you?"

Oooh.

Alfie jumped up. "Here we go again! Poor Stuart. Alfie's taking all his money." He paced, turning back to Stuart. "Write a fucking song, mate! You think what I do is so easy? Write a fucking song, then you can take your fair share."

Jett stood. "Gentlemen, let's take a breath here."

"She's been dead less than a week!" said Alfie. "If we do this, it's like spitting on her grave!"

"That might be fun," I said.

It took even me a moment to realize I was the one who said that.

They all turned and looked at me at once.

"Alice." said Jett.

Yes. Alice.

I climbed down the rest of the steps and walked over to them.

"Given how unwanted I was, that only seems fair," I said.

"I asked you to stay on the patio," said Jett.

"No, you suggested it," I said.

Stuart chuckled.

Jett sighed. "How much did you hear?"

"Enough," I said.

Jett pulled me aside. "Is it something you'd consider?"

I couldn't pry my eyes away from Alfie, mostly because he wouldn't quit staring at me. Man, that boy can glare.

Jett put his hands on either side of my face and made me look at him. "Would you do it?"

I nodded. "Sure."

That set Alfie off again. "Why the fuck would you want to do this? Revenge?"

Yes.

"Spite?"

Yes.

"Aren't you a bit old for mommy issues?" he said.

"I'm clearly not the only one who's still got issues with my mommy," I said.

He took a forceful step toward me. Jett stepped between us.

"Step back," said Jett.

Alfie knocked Jett's hand away and then turned away, distracting himself by lighting a cigarette. I turned too, kicking at the clutter from the fight, shaking my head. I could feel Alfie's eyes boring holes through the back of me.

"Thank you," said Jett. "Now, we need help—"

"I don't need her help," said Alfie.

Jett continued without acknowledging him. "And this is a potentially viable solution. Do you think you two can play nice for a few months?"

"Ask him," I said.

"Brat," Alfie retorted.

"I'm asking you both," said Jett.

I raised my right hand. "I swear on my mother's life."

"Alice!" hollered Jett.

Alfie is a quick little fucker. He was nearly on top of me before Jett stopped him short, yanking him back. Stephen got a shove in too. I laughed. Alfie struggled a moment and then shoved Jett away.

"You're gonna regret this, Little One," said Alfie. He said the last part pointedly, with as much vitriol as he could muster.

I'll admit it. Coming from his mouth, the nickname knocked me down a peg or two or ten. I didn't react to it, though. Fuck that guy. Again.

He glared at me like the cool guy he is until he was forced to blink and then stormed up the stairs.

TOXICOLOGY
—December 26, 2009

The *AP* is reporting Sara's official cause of death as "acute intoxication" by the combined effects of a bunch of different drugs—mainly painkillers and anti-anxiety meds—all of which she had prescriptions for.

They apparently got this information from the L.A. County coroner's office or maybe from the report the coroner's office released to the public, but nobody has contacted me about it. You'd think as her kid, someone would have made sure I was notified before the news went public but...nope. I'm still waiting for that call.

So, basically, the world's most beloved rock star died from taking too many pills.

What a fucking cliché.

She would have been 51 today.

PART TWO:
THE MIDDLE

WHAT WOULD SARA DO
—January 25, 2010

Holy fuck.

Interviews are annoying.

"What would Sara think about you joining this tribute, Alice?"

That's all any of them wants to know.

How the fuck would I know? I can't imagine she'd be thrilled. They must know that. How the hell am I supposed to answer that with any tact?

"I think she'd shit herself. I think she'd snort up a pile of cocaine, wash it down with some champagne, and then literally shit herself."

Jett tells me I can't answer like that though.

"Why are you doing this, Alice?"

"Spite. I'm doing this out of sheer spite. I'm taking her place in her precious band, beside her precious Alfie, specifically out of spite for her, spite for Alfie and spite for anybody else who ever had anything to do with this stupid fucking band and the hell I went through because of it."

Jett says I can't answer that way either.

He's always ruining my good time.

Everybody seems to think this is something of an organic undertaking. Sara was rock royalty, and now that she's gone, it's my time to take the throne. That's how they're approaching it in the media anyhow.

Does that make me Princess Alice?

The first person to call me that is getting dick punched.

I think it's a pretty ridiculous stance on things myself, but what the hell do I know? Jett's run away with it (of course he has; this whole thing was his idea), and Stuart has jumped on board. Stephen seems pretty ambivalent about the whole thing, which isn't horribly surprising.

And then there's Alfie. Alfie sees things very differently. Alfie sees me as a spiteful, entitled brat, and, let's face it, he might not be wrong about that, but people in glass houses and all that, Alfie. I've never seen a more coddled man in all my life, and my father is Stephen Moriarty.

What the hell have I gotten myself into?

The ceremony is still over two months away, and I'm already exhausted because of it. I've been holed up at my place with Jett for hours at a time practicing for these interviews and getting reprimanded for the questions I've already answered wrong.

Did you know that's a thing? Practicing for interviews. I didn't. Anyway, it's a thing for me. Jett goes over every question he can think of that I might be asked in the next onslaught of interviews, and we practice my responses. More accurately, he asks me these questions, and I answer them, and then he tells me my answers are inappropriate. It's become his new mantra: "That's inappropriate, Alice."

It's been super fun.

I think everybody's a bit worried I might ruin the whole "this is a tribute to Sara" thing.

The rest of my time, basically the time allotted for sleep, I've spent feverishly learning the lyrics to the *Wonderland* songs that I've very recently assured everybody I definitely know the lyrics to.

In my haste to piss off Alfie by agreeing to do this damn tribute, I've failed to recall that I know next to nothing about these songs. I have a vague knowledge of their more commercially successful songs. There was a time you couldn't go anywhere without hearing one of those fucking things on the radio. Their more obscure stuff is a complete mystery to me. Now, I have to learn them and learn them well enough to pass it off like I've known them all along.

I'm fucking beat.

No wonder Sara did so much coke.

Kidding! I'm kidding.

(But, seriously. No wonder.)

Want to hear a joke? Sara's lawyer stopped by not long after the memorial service. That's not the joke. What he brought with him, and the contents of said item, is the joke, and what he brought with him was Sara's will, inside of which it's stated that, in the event of her death, Sara's entire estate goes to her only child, Alice Moriarty.

That's me.

I'll give you a moment to let that sink in.

Yep. You're looking at the horrified new owner of Casa de Sara and everything in it. Or you would be if you were looking at me.

Right now, I'll bet you're asking yourself: Why would she leave everything to you when she couldn't go a day without wishing you were never born? That's an excellent question, one I asked Jett myself. As it turns out, the answer is fairly simple. It wasn't Sara who did it. It was Jett.

Jett convinced Sara to have a will drafted up a few years ago. I guess with all the reckless drinking and drug taking, he wasn't entirely convinced she'd make it to old age, and leaving an estate like Sara's without a designated heir was a potential legal nightmare he had no interest in dealing with. Also, had Chuck ever convinced Sara to marry him, as her surviving spouse, he would have gotten at least half of everything, if not all of it.

Sara wasn't great about the little things. The details. She let Jett take care of that. She trusted him. She knew he'd never allow her to sign anything that wasn't in her best interest, and rightly so. That never changed, not even after they divorced. He stayed on as her manager and financial advisor until the day she died. When Jett told her the will was okay to sign, she did it without question.

Now, he could have gone all Machiavellian and left it all to himself, but he didn't. How a man with Jett's integrity has survived working for decades in the immoral waste land that is the music industry is beyond me. He could have easily done it. With all the crap he's had to deal with over the last few decades, he could have taken it all for himself, and nobody would have said a word about it, certainly not me. But, instead, he named me as her sole beneficiary.

Talk about shitting herself...

Had Sara been buried instead of cremated she'd be rolling over in her grave right about now.

So, as sole beneficiary of her estate, not only do I get the house I hate, but I also get everything else: the contents of the house, the cars, all of her investments, all of her properties, and, most lucrative of all, the publishing rights to all of her songs. This includes the songs she wrote for *Wonderland*, more than half of which were co-written by Alfie.

This means Alice Moriarty and Alfie Evans are the proud new co-owners of some of the world's greatest music. This means any decision that ever has to be made regarding those songs has to be decided on by the both of us. Somebody wants to cover one of them? He can't say yes, unless I say yes. Somebody wants to use a song in a film? We have to decide together. I can say no when he says yes and yes when he says no just to be the immature brat he's constantly accusing me of being.

This could be fun.

Come to think of it, I should sue him for a percentage of the profits from "Little One" too. I've resigned myself to the fact that it's about me. It's only fair I get a cut of the profits.

Sarcasm alert: I definitely think that would make this whole situation less awkward and horrific.

Well, on to the next round of interviews. I hope they ask me what I think Sara would think about all of this!

SEE YOU BY THE STAIRS
—February 12, 2010

I stopped by Sara's house last night.

Well, my house, now, I guess.

It only took me two months to do it.

The quiet inside was jarring. Sara didn't like silence. The house was always loud. The noise distracted her voices, I think. My neurosis demands silence. My voices thrived in that noise. In that noise, they shouted things like, "everybody here hates you for breaking up the band" and, "if only you weren't born maybe things would be different for her."

My voices sounded an awful lot like Sara. Still do.

I hear them more and more these days but never more than when I look in the mirror. My eyes are Stephen's, but the rest...it's all Sara. It's always been this way, but it's different now that she's gone—now that people are asking me to take her place. It's as if a ghost stares back at me from the mirror.

The spirits of music and laughter and clinking glasses echoed off the marble walls as I made my way up the half-spiral staircase and down the hallway of photographs that don't include me.

Her bed was unmade, her journal lying facedown on the nightstand. She must have been staying there while the band was in town. The room expected her to return.

Sorry, it's just me now.

A stack of old photographs beside her journal caught my eye. It rested on December's issue of *Rolling Stone* magazine.

"Back Down the Rabbit Hole with Wonderland," said the cover.

My eyes rolled into the back of my head when I first saw that. When your name is Alice and your parents are in a famous band called *Wonderland*, the Alice in Wonderland puns pretty much vomit out of people wherever you go. There isn't one I haven't heard. For an extra chuckle, by sheer geographic happenstance—Sara lived in Laurel Canyon—the elementary school I went to was called Wonderland Avenue Elementary.

I'm not lying. Look it up.

Do you want to bet what will be on the cover of every fucking music publication in the world, if they go through with the rest of the tour with me after the Hall of Fame?

"Alice, in Wonderland."

You wait. I'll bet you anything.

Beneath the words on the cover of the *Rolling Stone*, the men of *Wonderland* gathered around a table dressed vaguely as Lewis Carroll's creations: Stephen in a chair studying a pocket watch; Stuart sprawled out on the table, eyes closed; Alfie in a bowtie and top hat brooding (of course) over a cup of tea.

The photo seemed to suggest that Stephen is the White Rabbit and that was baffling to me. Jett is the White Rabbit, hands down. Stephen is clearly the March Hare. ("Have some wine!") They nailed Stuart as the

Dormouse though ("I wasn't asleep...I heard every word you fellows were saying."), and Alfie as the Mad Hatter is a no-brainer.

At the head of the table sat Sara as the Red Queen. Of course.

"Off with their heads!"

That's actually the spot where Alice sat during the Mad Tea Party in the story, but whatever guys.

The cover got me thinking about that first reunion meeting. How awkward must that have been? The five of them in one room together. Sara had banged all but Stuart at some point over the years. She popped a kid out with one and married another. Do you think the boys secretly wondered which one was the best in her mind, sexually? Did each assume it was him? Did Sara ponder for herself which of them was the most passionate, tender, best kisser, etc.? Or were they actually professional about it?

Am I the only one thinking these thoughts?

And speaking of all this, why didn't Alfie freak out on Jett when Jett married Sara? Alfie didn't speak to Sara or Stephen for years after I was born, or after I was procreated, actually, but Alfie kept Jett on as his manager even after Jett married Sara. Why did Jett get a free pass from Alfie? No sense crying over spilled milk?

I hate my brain sometimes.

Where the hell was I?

There was a handwritten note wrapped around the stack of photos. They were photos of Sara and Alfie, obviously taken before they were famous. They were unrecognizable as the legendary rock stars they would become. Sara beamed at Alfie, her cheeks flush and full of baby fat. Alfie smiled back, his arm slung around her shoulders. Her eyebrows were bushy and unkempt. His black hair was thick and floppy, not stylishly disheveled like it is these days. Their teeth weren't nearly as straight or white. These were two kids who'd yet to be Hollywoodized.

They were just babies, really.

And so happy.

Why the hell was everybody so damn happy before I was born?

I never asked for any of this.

The note said: "Found these the other day. Hard to believe we were ever this young, isn't it? Glad we're doing this. Anyhow, see you by the stairs, Adams. Love, Alfie."

"See you by the stairs" was Alfie and Sara's little send off for one another when they were together, according to Jett. It referenced them meeting each other at the foot of the stairs that lead up to the stage before every show. In hindsight, it could also reference where it all eventually ended. It was at the foot of those stairs where Stephen attacked Alfie the night the band broke up.

The note bothered me. Since the age of five, I've been comforted by the fact that Alfie was a narcissistic asshole who couldn't handle the fact that Sara dared love anybody other than him. I'd convinced myself that she was better off without him, and so it was okay that he'd ditched her because of me. I've imagined my arrival as a white horse of sorts, rescuing her from his clutches.

The note (and the photos) was a tiny glimpse at a different Alfie Evans; evidence that perhaps he wasn't just a gloomy asshole.

I stuffed the note and photos in my bag and moved on to her walk-in closet. I clicked the light on and stepped inside. The closet was bigger than most homes. I walked down one side, pulling my hands through rows and rows of her clothing.

Against the wall at the back, a necklace dangling from a jewelry rack on her vanity caught my eye. Upon closer inspection, I found it had a sterling silver guitar pick pendent with a fingerprint etched into the silver. I put it around my neck and plopped one of Sara's hats on my head, examining myself in the mirror when something in the reflection caught my eye.

Behind me, shrouded by the long rack of clothes on the wall, was an antique trunk. I turned and ripped the clothes off the rack, throwing open the trunk. It was stacked full of Sara's leather journals.

No way.

Her journals are a constant in my memories of her. She was always writing in one. That a trunk full of journals existed wasn't a surprise to me. I thought she would have kept them sealed in a giant vault somewhere—there's certainly room enough for one on the premises—not right here in her closet for just anybody to stumble upon.

I couldn't imagine the things she'd written in them over the years. The things she'd said right to my face or within earshot of me were never all that great. I can't imagine what she wrote when she was alone with her thoughts.

I considered for a long while, six or seven seconds even, whether or not I should look through the journals, before deciding I would. I wish I was a bigger person. I really do. I wish I could have just closed that trunk, piled the clothes on top of it and walked away, forgetting about it forever. But, I'm not, and I didn't. I have an intrinsic and masochistic compulsion to be destroyed, it seems. To be destroyed by her.

I dug through the stack, assuming they were piled by year, and grabbed one from the very bottom. The journals dated back to the mid-seventies, more than a decade before I was born. She would have been younger than I am now when she started writing. I made a mental note before I moved on to my old room, to have the trunk picked up and delivered to my place.

My bedroom was the last one down the hall. Sometimes, I deluded myself into thinking this was because Sara was being considerate, because it was the farthest room from the noise downstairs. But I knew deep down she'd stashed me here because she wanted me as far away from her life as legally possible.

I cracked open the door and stepped inside. It had become little more than a storage area in the time since I'd lived there, which seemed kind of ridiculous given the size of that fucking house. There were tens of other rooms she could have thrown her junk in, but she choose this one. No surprise, really. It still smelled like my room though, like incense and cigarettes and shame.

As I wandered the room, the storage boxes and dust disappeared and were replaced by a memory of Jett outside my bathroom door that night. At the sound of shattering glass, he threw his body at that damn door over and over again.

That night, after Chuck dismounted me, I'd gone into my bathroom to clean up. I'd studied my reflection in the bathroom mirror, touching my battered face with uncoordinated hands. My lips were swollen and bruised, tank top torn, and there was a red handprint around my neck. The crook of my arm was bruised from clumsy needle marks.

If you ask her to choose, she'll choose me.

I'd ripped open the medicine cabinet and searched for a vial of coke. Sara had stashed them all over the house for safekeeping. Bottles of anxiety and depression meds and sleeping pills fell out and broke open as I hunted.

These pills were mine. A lifelong insomniac, Jett insisted on taking me to a specialist when I was twelve. I'd been prescribed every pill known to man by the time I was thirteen. A nervous child, they'd called me. I stopped taking the pills because the dreams I had when they finally put me to sleep were more horrific than my waking life. I preferred the hallucinations the insomnia sometimes brought. Plus, there was no fucking way in hell I was going to end up a pill-popping zombie like Sara.

I found some coke and uncapped it, sprinkling some of the powder into the hollow of my wrist behind my thumb, as I'd seen Sara and her "yes" people do over the years. I pressed one nostril closed and for the first time in my life, I snorted cocaine.

It burned. It burned bad, like I'd inhaled fire. That was okay. This pain was better than the alternative.

That was probably the decision that did me in that night. Cocaine is good for a lot of things but calming a person down is not one of them. It certainly wasn't good for quieting the voices.

Whiskey was good at calming me down. It didn't really quiet the voices but the voices entertained me when I drank, to a certain point, told me cute anecdotes and such. Shit, the heroin had been the most comforting experience of my life. Chuck could have left me a syringe full on the bedside table to help me deal with this fallout, like a considerate rapist/father-figure, but nooo.

Cocaine, though? Cocaine amplified everything.

That night, I slammed the cabinet door and examined my reflection again. Tears I hadn't realized I'd shed mixed with my eyeliner and left black channels down my cheeks. As I watched, the monster in the mirror began to sweat. Its blue eyes turned black.

My heart hammered against my rib cage.

"Be careful what you wish for," said the monster to me.

I slapped it. "Shut up!"

"Be careful what you wish for," it repeated.

I slapped it again, harder this time.

"Be careful what you wish for!"

"No!"

I slammed my hands into the glass until it broke, and the monster shut up.

Hands bleeding, I'd sunk to the floor and guzzled from a bottle I found lying by the toilet. At times, it was handy when random people passed out in your bathroom, especially when they left their booze behind. Times like when you're trying to be not alive for just a few moments.

I scooped up a handful of the scattered pills and swallowed them, and then a second and then a third, until the effects of the cocaine dulled. My vision blurred. I was vaguely aware of Jett's voice and the thump of his body against the door, but it all seemed so far away. Sweat mixed with blood mixed with tears. The voices screamed at me.

You're trapped. This is your life now.

Not even the pills silenced the voices.

A glint of light rebounded off a piece of the broken mirror on the floor next to my hand and caught my eye. I picked it up, dug it into my wrist and dragged it across my skin.

It didn't even hurt. The blood was immediate, and it was everywhere.

I don't know how long it took for me to pass out. I don't know how long it took Jett to get through the door, but I do know the last time I left that room I was in Jett's arms, and I was dying.

I walked out of that room, went back into the master bedroom and did something I'd never done before. I crawled into Sara's bed and fell asleep.

TELL ME
—March 1, 2010

The 2010 Rock and Roll Hall of Fame induction ceremony will be held in New York City on April 5. Our first week of rehearsals was last week, and it went really well.

Just kidding!

It was awful.

As it turns out, and this will come as a huge surprise to you, Alfie and I don't get along. At all. The original confrontation at Stephen's house wasn't a meet-cute like in the movies where the main characters hate each other at first but slowly come to realize they only hate each other because they're so in love.

This is definitely not that.

He definitely despises my existence, and I can't stand the sight of his stupid face, handsome as it may be.

Ugh.

The tribute will be a ten-minute performance of a blend of some of Sara's most popular songs. Songs she wrote with *Wonderland* and songs from her solo career. It's a lot to remember, and these rehearsals have shed a giant, fucking spotlight on the fact that I don't know the songs as well as I've led everybody to believe. I can see Jett giving me the look. Every time I screw up a lyric or miss one of my cues, he pops his head up from the never-ending pile of paperwork on his lap, and I can feel it, the look.

If they think this is bad, they should have seen me two months ago! I've made significant improvement since then. Is it my fault I lied to them?

Don't answer that.

This is a lot of shit to learn in a short amount of time, even if I had known the lyrics by heart: cues and beats and timing, where to stand, where not to stand, when to move, when not to move. It's a lot to keep track of. I'm used to one tiny stage with one microphone, one guitar, and one person. Me.

Now I've got to keep track of myself and three other people. Thankfully, Stuart doesn't move, and Stephen barely moves, but Alfie never stops moving. I swear he's even tried to trip me with the cable on his guitar. He can't wait for the next time I fuck up so he can say "I told you so" to everybody again.

Alfie finally lost it on me today. It was inevitable. He'd been on edge all day. Actually, he always seems to be on edge. He may want to consider adding more fiber to his diet.

I wonder if he was born that way. Did he come out of the chute with a cigarette dangling from his lips, glowering at the doctor for ripping him from the solitude of the womb?

Today, he seemed particularly edgy, and so was I.

"Fuck," I said, for about the billionth time this week. "Sorry."

"S'alright," said Stuart. "Let's go again."

Alfie muttered something that sounded like "unfucking believable."

I turned to him. "You have something to say to me?"

"You don't want to know what I have to say," he muttered.

"Don't hold back on my account," I said.

He locked his eyes on me for a moment and then exploded. "Why the fuck are you doing this? You don't even know the fucking songs!"

Well, I asked for it, didn't I? A running theme in my life...

"It's rehearsal!" I said. "Either I fuck it up here or I fuck it up live. Which would you prefer?"

"I'd prefer you didn't fuck it up at all," he said. "This is Wonderland, Princess. The big time. This isn't open mic night at the corner fucking bar."

Princess.

My jaw clamped down so tightly I felt the tension in my neck. Fortunately for him, he wasn't close enough for me to dick punch.

I drew in a breath and released it slowly. "Does it make you feel better to hate me?"

It was a sincere question. For a man with seemingly so much else to be bitter about, you'd think he'd ease up a bit—perhaps understand I got just as raw a deal as he did?

But, nooo.

"I don't care enough about you to hate you," he said.

He nailed it. Maximum hurt, minimum energy expended. You're not important enough to hate, silly girl. You're just a gnat. Annoying, for sure, but not worth enough to hate.

He'd taken a page right out of Sara's playbook for that one.

Great minds think alike.

Stuart thumped on his bass drum. "Enough."

I looked to the floor and turned my head away. Alfie's weight shifted from one foot to the other and back again in my watery, peripheral vision. Stephen put his hand on my shoulder, but I knocked it away. The last thing I wanted or needed was pity from that guy.

Alfie brought his hands to his hips and then tucked them to his chest. It felt like he was waiting for me to say my tears weren't for what he'd said. But fuck him. Find absolution elsewhere, asshole.

I wiped my eyes with the back of my hand and sniffed. "You really think you'd have lived happily ever after with her if I was never born?"

"Just forget it," said Alfie, as he tried to turn away.

"You won't let me!" I shouted.

He faced me again with a sigh and an eye roll, crossing his arms again.

"Your life together was so perfect that she fucked your best friend? Why? Just to spice things up a bit?" I said. "You'd still be together now if I didn't exist, is that it?"

He said nothing. He looked bored. I think that's what did it. He had the nerve to look bored.

I stepped to him and shoved him. "Is that it?"

His arms fell to his sides. His mouth dropped open, and his face clouded over. The muscles of his jaw rippled under his skin.

Jett popped up from his seat in front of the stage, and the papers in his lap cascaded to the floor.

"You guys would be, what, sitting together on your front porch swing right now?" I asked. "Answer me!"

I shoved at him again, but this time he knocked my arms away and shoved me back.

I charged him, slamming him against a set of giant speakers by Stuart. The speakers fell into his drums, and Stuart leaped off his kit before he got caught in the avalanche. Alfie lost his footing and fell to the floor. My momentum sent me to the floor beside him.

I continued to attack before he could get his bearings, climbing over top of him, swinging and clawing at him. Alfie blocked the blows with his arms, but some of them landed.

"You'd be on your swing, behind your perfect picket fence, with your perfect children and your perfect dogs?" I yelled. "Tell me how it would be!"

He finally caught hold of my wrists and rolled, coming up on top of me, pinning my arms on either side of my head. His guitar, which was still strapped to his body, clunked on the floor beside us and made an awful screeching noise through the amp.

"Stop," he said, breathless. His cheeks puffed out as he panted, still fighting to contain me. "Stop it."

But I didn't want to stop. I didn't want him to stop. I wanted him to fight back so I could rail against him. It was the one time I actually wanted him to be a nasty, son of a bitch, and he denied me.

In fact, his expression turned almost despondent.

He finally caught my flailing legs with his feet and clamped down on them. I was forced to be still.

Stephen yanked Alfie away from me. I scrambled to my feet and went after Alfie again, but Jett had reached the stage by then and caught me, mid-lunge.

"Let me go," I said, struggling. "Let me go!"

He lost his grip on me for a second, and I lunged again, but Stephen stepped in front of Alfie, and my hand hit his chest instead. When it rebounded, he grabbed my wrist and held it still.

Seeing this, seeing Stephen step in to protect Alfie, was an eye-opener. Christ, Stephen was the first to beat on Alfie, and there he was stepping in to protect the man from me.

So I stopped. Everything just kind of stopped. We stood there still, like wax figures in a museum.

Stephen released me cautiously. He and Alfie both watched me with wide eyes. Red scratches marked Alfie's neck and chest. I glanced at Jett over my shoulder. His eyes matched theirs. So did Stuart's.

"Can I go?" I asked Jett.

He hesitated, but nodded.

I walked off stage.

That ended the first week of rehearsals for the new and decidedly unimproved *Wonderland*.

LIKE HELL YOU ARE
—March 5, 2010

One week down, one month to go.

This damn tribute has triggered something in me. I've started to examine my past in a way I haven't done before, and I'm not sure how I feel about what I'm finding. I remember things now I don't remember having memory of before she died. Is that normal?

I was five, about to turn six, when Jett finally had enough and decided to leave Sara. I watched from the staircase as Jett trudged through the remains of the party. A black garbage bag trailed behind him like Linus's blanket. I could tell he had barely enough energy to stand, let alone clean. He'd just gotten home from the final leg of a six-month tour for Alfie's latest solo endeavor. The bottles, glasses, garbage, and an untouched buffet of now rotting food must have seemed insurmountable. Yet, he powered through.

Sara was curled up on the couch with a blanket over her legs writing in her journal, ignoring Jett. Her indifference was her way of punishing him for accompanying Alfie on his tour. Apathy was Sara's go-to response to everything that pissed her off. That this was his profession, his livelihood, that he had also accompanied her on her last tour that ended only days before Alfie's began, meant nothing to her. Her husband had betrayed her, plain and simple.

"Where's Alice?" asked Jett.

Sara said nothing.

"I thought we agreed no more parties while I'm away?" said Jett.

Sara shrugged.

"Did you bother to check on her last night?" asked Jett. "Or this morning?"

She continued to write.

"Do you have any idea if she's even here, Sara? Whether or not she's hungry? Thirsty? Breathing?"

"We both know you've checked on her already," said Sara finally. "She's fine. Stop with the dramatics."

Jett hurled a glass at the wall above Sara.

Sara cried out and shielded her head, leaping up to escape falling glass "Jesus Christ, Jett!"

"You don't deserve the title of mother," he said.

Sara laughed. "I've been telling you that for years! You're just now figuring that out?"

Jett dropped the bag and sat on the couch where Sara had been, hanging his head. His rage contained as quickly as it erupted, he brushed the back of his fingers against his cheek.

Sara sat beside him.

"Did he stay here while I was gone?" said Jett.

"Who?" said Sara.

"You know who."

At the time, I didn't know who he meant. It couldn't have been Chuck yet. There were quite a few before Chuck moved in.

Jett lifted his head and looked at Sara. His normally bright eyes were dull, bloodshot, and so very sad.

Sara studied him, perhaps considering a lie, but she'd never been able to lie to his face. Instead, she shrugged.

"I thought so," said Jett.

There was a heavy inevitability in his voice. He knew this night would come.

"You knew what you were getting into when you married me," said Sara.

"Did I?"

"Nobody asked you to marry me," said Sara, her eyes brimming with tears. She wiped them quickly. "You only married me because of her, Jett. If we're being honest, let's be honest."

He looked away, taking in a deep breath. He dragged himself to his feet and picked at the broken glass, gingerly placing the larger pieces in the garbage bag.

"I'm sorry for this," he said. "I haven't slept in days."

Sara shrugged.

I knew then what came next. I, too, knew this night would come.

You see, this is what I'm talking about. At not even six years old, could I really have understood that that night would come, that Jett would give up and leave us? It doesn't seem possible, does it?

Because I think it must have been a huge, fucking surprise. It pretty much crushed me.

Why am I remembering it now like I knew it was coming?

"I'll find a place of my own tomorrow," said Jett.

Sara picked at her nails. "Surprise, surprise."

"And I'm taking her with me."

Sara's eyes darted to him. "Like hell you are."

Jett sighed.

"She's not yours to take," continued Sara. "If you want to leave, then leave. But you're leaving us both behind."

"So you're going to hold me hostage, then?" said Jett. "Like you've held yourself hostage for the past half decade? Won't you ever forgive yourself?"

Sara folded her arms and sat back, looking to the floor.

He knelt before her. "Do you think he's still torturing himself after all these years?" said Jett. "I can tell you he isn't. He's moved on. He's living his life. You need to do the same."

Sara looked at him, dark eyes wide and searching, and for a moment, I saw who she used to be before I came along. I understood why so many loved her.

But did I really? I was on the staircase, after all. I could just barely hear them, let alone see them. How could I have seen her eyes so clearly?

I'm starting to think I've invented many of my memories, or embellished them, at a minimum.

What else have I invented in my mind?

The following morning, I sat near the bottom of the stairs and watched as Jett made his way past me with a bag full of his clothes. He set the bag near the front door and took a moment before he turned to me. His eyes were red.

"Come here," he said, crouching to my level.

I didn't. I knew if I went to him he would say goodbye, and then he would be gone. I didn't want him to leave. Maybe if I just stayed put, he'd have to stay put too.

Jett straightened and walked to the steps, sitting beside me.

"I know you don't understand any of this," he said.

But I understood just fine.

He shifted so he was crouched in front me and held out his hands, palms up. My frown faded, and I tried to slap his hands. He moved them at the last second and made an "O" with his thumb and forefinger, holding his fingers to his eye.

"Too slow, Cherrio."

I giggled.

"That's my girl," he said, and his eyes grew very sad.

I put my arms around his shoulders.

He held me tightly and whispered through his tears, "I promise I'll be back for you. I'll always come back for you."

Sara wandered in then. Her eyes were wet and red like Jett's.

"You're still here?" she said to Jett.

Jett wiped his eyes and stood, facing her. I grabbed Jett's finger and watched Sara from behind his leg.

"Please let me take her," he said.

"She's not yours to take," said Sara.

"She doesn't belong here, Sara," said Jett. "You know that."

"Alice, come here," said Sara, gesturing for me.

I moved farther behind Jett.

"Oh, for Christ's sake," said Sara.

She pushed Jett aside and lifted me awkwardly into her arms. I think it was the first time she'd ever held me, at least that I could remember. It felt very unnatural. I stiffened and leaned away from her.

"This is what you wanted, Jett," said Sara. "You want to leave, so leave. We'll be just fine on our own, won't we?"

I'm pretty sure it was a rhetorical question, but even at five years old I knew we would not be just fucking fine on our own. Christ. It was a nightmare.

Jett hesitated. Sara wiggled her wedding ring from her finger and launched it at him. It bounced off his chest and hit the floor.

"Always hated that thing anyhow," she said.

Jett ignored her, speaking directly to me. "I'll come back."

"Get out!" Sara shouted.

He left.

They were divorced soon after. Jett was no longer my stepfather, and I was alone in that house with Sara. It was that same week I saw Alfie for the first time.

I can't stop thinking about Alfie tonight. I can't stop thinking about that look in his eyes the other night at rehearsal, the sadness in them as he struggled to restrain me. I think back to that night I first saw him, when he freaked out and ran away, and I remember now seeing it in his eyes then, too.

Don't I?

I fear I'm going mad.

ACCUSATION
—April 3, 2010

Do you know how excruciating a flight from Los Angeles to New York is with your estranged, dead mother's unstable ex-boyfriend glaring at you the entire time?

Alfie is like a Saturday Night Live character. I mean, rock stars out of their natural habitat are a ridiculous bunch anyhow, but this guy takes it to extremes. And he's a bit too stuck in the eighties, if you ask me, with his spiffy jackets and tee shirts and man scarves and hair.

Okay, to be honest, he actually looks pretty good most of the time. He's kind of strikingly attractive, speaking strictly of his physical looks. You won't tell him I said that, will you?

I brought the journal from her nightstand with me on the trip to New York. What better way to ramp up some much needed confidence than by obsessing over your dead mother's journal, in which she doesn't mention you at all?

I could feel Alfie's eyes on me as I read it on the plane. He must have known it was her journal. They all look the same and they span three decades. I'm sure she wrote in them in his presence when they were together.

I bet he'd love to get his hands on it and read what she wrote. I'll bet he wonders if she kept writing about him after the break-up. If I were nice I'd let him look at it.

If I were nice.

The answer to that question is yes, by the way. Yes, she kept writing about him after the break-up. This journal alone is infested with him, and it's the most recent one.

After six hours of ignoring Alfie, we reached New York. From the tarmac, we were corralled into a set of limousines—me, Stuart and Jett in one; Alfie and Stephen in the other. The limos shuttled us to the hotel that would be our home for the next three nights.

I wasn't prepared for the blitz of fans that were waiting for us there. It was like showing up with The Beatles. Girls younger than me and women older than them threw themselves at the boys, and each girl had her favorite.

Stuart is a modern-day hippie. Kind of. His version is slightly less organic than an actual hippie—he spends a lot of time on his appearance, making it look like he spends no time at all. Don't tell him I told you that. Stuart is the rock star for dreamy, poetic groupies.

Stephen is...well, he's Stephen. I'm not going to go into too much detail about the attractiveness of my father. He's tallish. Lean. He's clean, but he often looks unwashed. Very rock star like. He's the rock star for dirty girls looking to get back at daddy.

Alfie is the requisite dreamboat of the group—the eyes, the hair, the attitude, plus he's a guitarist, and you get added points for that on the groupie scale of fame. I'd say Alfie got about fifty percent of the attention and Stuart and Stephen split the remaining fifty. Nobody gave a shit about me.

The boys took it in stride, as if it was the most natural thing in the world for them, and I suppose it was. They've been rock stars more than half their lives, much longer than they haven't been. It was all new to me, though.

And do you want to know one of the most mortifying places a girl can find herself? Smack dab in the middle of a hormone-fueled free-for-all for her father and his buddies.

A bunch of the fans were wearing tee shirts with Sara on them, Diary. Shirts from *Wonderland* concerts way back when, shirts from her last solo tour, and everything in between.

All of them watched me with sidelong accusations as I walked past them and into the hotel.

INSIGHT
—April 4, 2010

Less than one day to go. By tomorrow it will be all over with, the Hall of Fame.

Also, life as I know it.

My nerves are shot.

I shouldn't be reading Sara's journal. I know that. I think a part of me hoped I'd find something inside it to help me through this performance, but no such luck. If this journal was the only historical record of Sara's life, nobody in generations to come would ever know she had a child. I haven't gotten to the rest of them yet, but I can't imagine I make many appearances in any of them either.

I was sprawled on my bed, flipping through the journal and muttering to myself like a crazy person, when someone knocked at the door. Before I could respond, Jett poked his head inside, eyes closed.

"You decent?" he said.

I dropped the journal to the mattress. "You have a key to my room?"

"Mmm hmm," he said. "Rules of the road."

"It's not the road yet," I said. "Is it?"

"Close enough," he said. "Are you decent?"

"How long will you stand there like that if I don't answer you?"

He brought out his stern voice. "Alice."

I rolled my eyes. "Define decent."

"Clothed? No drugs or boys?"

"Fully-clothed, no boys," I said. "Give me a sec to hide the drugs though."

His eyes popped opened and looked around. "Not funny."

I smiled.

He crossed the room and stood over me. "How're you feeling?"

"Oh, you know. Terrified. Horrified. Unqualified," I said. "All the bad 'ifieds.'"

"You're hardly unqualified," he said, tilting his head to look at the journal. "What's that?"

"Nothing."

"Her journal?"

I nodded.

"So, something, then," he said.

He picked up the journal and sat beside me. I fought the urge to grab it from him. I knew he'd tell me to stop reading it, and then I'd have nobody but myself to blame if I didn't listen and became (more) damaged because of it.

His eyes scanned the pages, and I bit the inside of my cheek.

"Jesus," he muttered. "Where'd you find this?"

"On her nightstand."

"I'm not sure you should be reading this," he said.

I shrugged. "It's some pretty good insight."

"Insight or insanity?"

"Insight into insanity?" I said.

He looked at me. "That's a great name for an album."

I chuckled. Despite his best efforts, Jett was never not a manager. He can't help himself.

"Better get me through tomorrow before you line me up for an album," I said.

"You're going to do fine tomorrow," he said, going back to his reading. I think even Jett was curious about what she wrote.

I flopped back on the bed and stared up at the ceiling. "I'm going to fuck it up."

"You're not going to fuck it up."

"I'm going to fuck it up, and I'll finally be revealed as the fraud I am," I muttered.

Jett clamped the book shut and set it down. "Well, if you do fuck it up, you can always try your hand at acting. You have a certain flair for the melodramatic."

I lifted my head and narrowed my eyes at him.

"Listen to me," he said. I dropped my head back to the mattress. He sighed. "Would you please listen to me? Come on, sit up."

I did, begrudgingly.

"You are not going to fuck it up," said Jett. "And you are not a fraud. Why do you think that?"

"Besides the fact that I hated her, and I don't know a thing about her music, yet I'm basically the one headlining this fucking thing?"

"Language," said Jett. "And I don't believe you really hated her, Alice."

I gave him one of my looks, and he wisely moved on.

"Look, you know the music," he said. "You had a bumpy start, but you know it now. You're going to do just fine."

"And the fraud part?" I asked.

He considered. "Nobody but me, you and maybe your father knows the true extent of the issues between you and Sara," he said. "Nobody out there will think you're a fraud."

I wanted to tell him even he didn't know the true extent of the issues, but I didn't. That can of worms was best left unopened and buried.

"I have to wrangle up the others and get them into bed at a decent hour," said Jett. "Are you going to be okay?"

"Yeah."

"Are you sure?"

I nodded.

"Positive?"

"Yes! Jett, I'm fine," I said. "Go."

"Okay, okay. Call me if you need anything?"

I nodded.

"And stop reading that thing, at least for tonight. Get some sleep?"

Pfft.

I nodded again.

"Goodnight," he said.

"Goodnight."

As soon as the door closed behind him, I started reading again.

I CAN'T DO THIS
—April 5, 2010

Oh, God.
I can't do this.
Please, don't make me do this.

DRINK ME
—April 6, 2010

Thanks to the nice people at Second Fucking Chances rehabilitation clinic, I've been sober since I was fifteen. According to them, if you "eliminate alcohol and all other substances" from your life you also magically expel all your problems from your life. (I'm sure there's more to it than that, but I wasn't really paying attention.)

Poof! No more apathetic mother.

Ta-dah! No more drunken father.

Abracadabra! Rape? Never even happened!

To be fair, Sara has indeed been expelled from my life but only because of booze and drugs.

Explain that one, Second Fucking Chances.

After a night of no sleep because of rational and irrational anxiety, I decided that right before the Hall of Fame performance was the perfect time to tumble off the wagon.

My thirst for booze started in the press line. Do you know what a press line is? I didn't. I mean, I had a vague understanding of it. I'd been to industry events before. Jett used to take me to them when he and Sara were married. I'd never been down one of them though. Not until last night.

A press line is a God-forsaken place that famous people are led through, one by one, like sheep through a barn door.

First, you're directed by a handler you've never met, who calls you by your first name, to stand and stay where he or she points. (Stand. Stay. Good girl! Want a treat?) You're forced to plaster a smile on your face while you're blinded by the flashes from what seems like a thousand cameras, while the people behind the cameras shout a bunch of crap at you.

"Over here, Alice!"

"Over your shoulder!"

"Look at me!"

"This way!"

Your smile becomes more faked by the second, and you struggle not to blink, because closed eyes and half-closed eyes in photos could be potential fodder for headlines you'd rather not read about yourself.

"Alice Moriarty Drunk at Hall of Fame?"

Not yet.

From there you're pushed down a seemingly endless stream of journalists, video and print, who ask you the same fucking questions.

"What's it like to be here tonight?"

"What have these last few months been like for you?"

"Have you learned anything from this experience?"

"What do you think Sara would say about all this?"

I literally cannot escape that last question.

They each become bored with you at about the same time, as they spot someone trailing behind you in the procession; someone they think will be more interesting than you. For me, this was Alfie, of course. I was shuttled down the line between him and Stephen. I couldn't really hear the questions they were asked or their answers, but I heard my name several times, from behind me and in front.

I could barely breathe by the time I escaped the gauntlet. Jett took me to what would be my dressing room for the night, a tiny room big enough for only a couple chairs and a small table. Prone to pacing, I could take only three steps before turning around, and I could only do that if I shoved the chairs under the table.

Like a teenager, the second Jett was out of eyesight, I grabbed the first person I spotted and asked him to get me a bottle of something, anything, alcoholic. I don't know if this was his job. In fact, it most certainly wasn't his job, but he came through like a champ. He appeared only minutes later with a full bottle of whiskey in hand.

Was there a liquor store there?

I hope this doesn't mean I'm becoming a diva.

I said thank you and offered him some, but he politely declined. He was at work, after all. I assume. Then again, so was I.

I poured myself a small glass and stared at it. An internal battle ensued. It went something like this:

Drink it.

Don't drink it.

No, drink it.

No, don't drink it.

Compelling stuff.

I got the glass all the way to my lips before I turned and dumped it on the floor with a growl.

Jesus, I dumped it on the floor.

And I didn't clean it up.

I am becoming a diva.

I refilled and held the glass up, eyeing it like it was standing opposite me at high noon at the O.K. Corral. I brought it to my lips two or three times and balked each time and then laughed at myself.

I looked up at the ceiling, talking directly to Sara now, "You laughing yet?"

"She ever answer you?"

I whirled around, the whiskey sloshing over the rim and down my arm.

Alfie leaned against the doorway, arms crossed, the door propped open by his booted foot. He was stage-ready except for last minute tucks and buttonings. He wore tailored, pinstripe pants jammed into elaborate laced and buckled combat boots, a white dress shirt rolled at the sleeves and unbuttoned to his sternum and an unbuttoned suit vest over top.

The Mad Hatter himself.

The rolled cuffs revealed previously-unseen-by-me tattoos on his forearms. The phrase "SEA of Love" etched in an artfully-designed heart on his left arm was hard to miss.

SEA: Sara Elizabeth Adams.

His eyeliner made his dark gaze pop and would've looked ridiculous on any other man, especially a man well into his 50s. On Alfie, though, it fit. He looked...hot.

Ugh.

"Jesus," I said, hoping he took it as simple surprise and not awe.

He took in my reaction and smirked. I'm not fond of smirks, in general. I was reminded of another smirk from another doorway. This one didn't disgust me though.

"Sorry," he said.

I gulped back the whiskey, wincing as I swallowed. "You don't look sorry," I squeaked out through the burn of the alcohol in my throat.

I'd forgotten how much I like that burn.

He shifted his foot and let the door close behind him. It shut out the noise in the hallway. I was left with deafening silence. Deafening silence and Alfie, and in that moment, I understood why Sara had surrounded herself with noise.

I watched his short approach more warily than I'd eyed the alcohol moments before. Whiskey was an old friend. This was an old nemesis on approach, my beautiful kryptonite in eyeliner and combat boots.

And my mother's initials etched into his skin.

He stopped just short and looked down at me. His boots were slightly heeled, and I was barefoot so he loomed over me in a way he hadn't before.

The silence grew louder. We hadn't ever been alone before. It was a weird sensation. In him, I see Sara. It's inescapable. And I think it's safe to say the same is true for him when he looks at me. Together, we're like the ghost of Sara looking at her reflection through some cosmic mirror.

He finally broke the silence. "So, does she ever answer you?"

"Of course not."

"Me either," he said. "Nervous?"

I answered too quickly, defensively. "No."

He sighed.

I didn't appreciate that sigh.

"Why are you here?" I asked. "Don't you have some inappropriately-aged groupies to attend to?"

He dipped his chin and turned his head a notch, gazing at me somewhat sidelong. "No."

The power of that gaze was...well, powerful. I couldn't tear my eyes away. Awkward as I am, I'm often at a loss for words (outside the rambling mutterings of this diary), but this left me at a loss for even thoughts.

Let's call this the Evans Effect.

"Anyhow, that's more your father's hobby," he said.

That snapped me out of it, and I groaned. "You had to say that?"

He chuckled. "Relax. There aren't any groupies here tonight. This is a classy establishment."

What had gotten into him? He was treating me like an actual human being, not like a splinter that had been festering under his skin for decades.

"Why are you being so nice to me?" I asked. "Did you lose a bet or something?"

He laughed again. "No, but I am a bit drunk."

Ah. Alcohol.

Cheers!

His eyes drifted to my necklace, the one I found at Sara's place. He stepped closer and lifted the pendant, lifted it directly from my skin. The Evans Effect increases exponentially with physical contact, as it turns out. At the risk of sounding like an airport romance novel, his fingertips blazed a trail across my skin and sent goose bumps up my spine. I refuse to divulge, however, what, if anything, it did to my loins.

"What is it?" I asked.

"I gave this to her," he said, brushing his thumb over the silver. "It's my fingerprint."

"Oh," I replied, very poetically.

"Where'd you find it?"

"At Sara's place," I said. "On her vanity."

"The one in her closet?" he asked.

I nodded, eyebrows furrowing. "You know it?"

"I did live there for years," he said.

"You did?"

It dawned on me then that I knew nothing about the history of that house, except what I had lived through. Like it hadn't existed before I did.

Maybe I'm a narcissist.

He looked at me. "You didn't know that? You two didn't talk?"

It was my turn to laugh. "You really were left out of the loop, weren't you?" I said. "No, Sara took more of an ignore-it-and-maybe-it-will-go-away approach to parenting."

I stepped past him and poured another drink, a foolish thing to do. I was barely prepared for this performance as it was. I certainly didn't need anything hindering my senses.

"I'm sorry," he said.

"For what?" I turned back to him.

He considered a moment but then shrugged. "I should go."

He was gone as quickly as he arrived.

Some time (and drinks) later, I was retrieved by a handler and escorted to the backstage area, which was swarming with musicians, inductees and presenters alike. You'd think as the child of rock stars, I wouldn't be intimidated by other rock stars, but this is inaccurate. Not that it mattered. Nobody seemed to even realize who the hell I was. A few did a double-take when they saw me, all men. Probably men she'd banged over the years, thinking they'd spotted a ghost.

I peaked around the curtain at the crowd. More rock stars, more famous people. I let the curtain fall away and turned my back on it, the panic setting in.

"In another moment down went Alice after it," I muttered, quoting one of my favorite lines from Lewis Carroll's masterpiece, a masterpiece this band had long ago bastardized. "Never once considering how in the world she was to get out again."

"Talking to yourself?" asked Stuart, appearing beside me and throwing on a dress shirt. There was a necktie jammed in his jeans pocket. "Not a good sign."

He watched me pace as he buttoned his shirt. "You're going to cut a channel in the floor."

"Either I pace or I puke," I said.

"I threw up on stage once," he said, tugging his collar like a six year old, struggling with the tie. He gave up and yanked open the top buttons, tossing the tie away. "It was more because of the whiskey than nerves though."

"You're not helping."

If I were a writer, this would be a great spot for a plot twist.

Chuck Wall slithered into view over Stuart's shoulder, about twenty yards away. I thought I imagined him at first, assuming the voices had graduated into hallucinations. So I blinked. And I blinked again, but still he remained, talking with a small group of handlers, who fussed at his clothes and patted his face with makeup.

"What the hell's he doing here?" I asked.

Stuart glanced over his shoulder and rolled his eyes. "He's inducting us."

"What?"

"I'm not happy about it either, but he produced all our albums," said Stuart. "He gets to induct us."

I stared at Stuart, mouth attractively (I'm sure) agape, unable to fathom how this moment had come to transpire. I often forget that nobody else knows the truth about what Chuck did to me. I chose to keep this information to myself so my reality was very different from everybody else's.

Still. Chuck was a creep who'd kept Sara doped up for years, and everybody knew that, at least in that fucked-up little circle. Why, then, had they allowed this? How could they allow him to speak about her?

The voices said to me then that people could ask the same thing about me, about my relationship with Sara, about my performing in this tribute to her.

Fuck off, voices.

I stepped past Stuart, eyes focused on Chuck.

"Uh oh," said Stuart. He tried to grab me, but I dodged him, approaching Chuck quickly.

Chuck's expression faltered when he spotted me. He, too, saw a ghost, I'm sure. But then his disgusting mouth formed a huge grin. "Alice! How lovely to see you again, my dear-"

I shoved him. "You bastard!"

Representatives from the biggest publications in the music industry were floating around backstage. The camera flashes were almost instantaneous. In the back of my mind, I knew it was a bad idea and that I should stop, but I didn't have that ability. Not in that moment.

"How dare you show your face here?" I spat, shoving him again.

He grabbed my wrists to restrain me, yanking me toward him in the process. I lost my footing and toppled into him, and I'm sure that was his intention. He put his arms around me to steady me, just like he had that night.

He still smelled the same as he did all those years ago, too, Diary, like whiskey and something rotten. I was transported back to that night, and I freaked out.

"Let go of me!" I screamed, struggling.

Stuart jumped in and pulled at his arms. "Let her go!"

"I'm only trying to keep her from falling over," Chuck said, much too calmly. "Looks like somebody got into the bottle a bit too early."

Chuck laughed, and others joined him, until he yelped and lost his grip me. Stuart caught me and steadied me, and I turned, shocked to find Alfie yanking Chuck away from me by his neck.

He threw Chuck up against the wall and stared him down, his back straight, chest out, like a provoked alpha lion.

Chuck immediately stood down, holding up his hands defensively.

Alfie backed away slowly. "Coward."

Cameras continued to record.

Cheers from the clueless crowd signaled Chuck's cue. Chuck adjusted his clothing and straightened his tie, eyes still on Alfie. His handlers soon whisked him away to the stage.

Alfie turned to me. "You ok?"

I nodded a lie.

He looked me over and put his hand on my cheek. "You're shaking."

Evans Effect to the rescue. I calmed considerably.

"Whoops, hand check," whispered Stuart, elbowing Alfie. "Dad's on deck."

Alfie shot him a look and dropped his hand. My anxiety materialized again, like flowers out of a magician's top hat. I looked over my shoulder as Jett and Stephen appeared.

"Alice, do you want to talk about what just happened?" said someone I didn't recognize, jamming a recorder in my face.

"What?" I said.

"What? What just happened?" asked Jett.

"We could sit down and..."

Stuart shoved the man in his face. "Go away."

Cheers arose again from the crowd. The lights dimmed. I remembered again why we were all here.

"Oh fuck," I said.

Stuart smacked me on the butt like he was a gym coach. "No turning back now, love."

It was like a fucking nightmare. No, it was a fucking nightmare come to life.

Trailing behind the other three, I tried to follow a bouncing beam of light from somebody's flashlight as we walked out on stage, but it made me dizzy. Instead, I focused on the shimmer from a piece of silver on one of Alfie's boots.

Alfie and Stephen shook hands at center stage and then separated, off to their respective microphones. Stuart loped off to his drum kit. When Alfie hit a practice chord, the cheers grew louder, and I froze in place.

Rehearsal was one thing. Rehearsal was in front of nobody. This was much different. There were hundreds in the crowd, maybe thousands, and millions more would eventually see it at home. Millions of people who loved Sara. Millions of people who would take one look at me and shake their heads.

Poor imitation of her mother.

Fraud.

Opportunist.

The voices nodded their concurrence.

Alfie was beside me then, offering me his hand. I looked at it and then grabbed it as if it were a lifeline.

He squeezed it gently. "Breathe, Alice."

I hadn't even realized I'd been holding my breath. I exhaled.

Evans Effect to the rescue, again.

"Don't forget to breathe," he said, escorting me to my microphone. "If you get lost, look at me."

I nodded. He kissed the side of my head. A murmur rolled through the crowd closest to the stage and through the voices in my head. We were all just beginning to contemplate the significance of that kiss when Stuart counted off four beats, and the guys launched into the first song.

I very nearly missed my first cue, as I had so many times in rehearsals. Almost. That's all that counts. I have no idea what the performance looked like, but I didn't miss that fucking cue, and I got all the lyrics exactly right.

I got them right, Diary, and if that performance was ten minutes it was ten hours.

We were supposed to gather together at center stage while the crowd heaved accolades at us, and stood to honor Sara with, what was sure to be, a thunderous applause. I was uncomfortable with that idea all along. Singing her songs was one thing. Accepting praise for it was another.

So as the performance concluded, I turned and headed off stage. As I did, a giant photograph of Sara, ten meters high, appeared on the screen in back and illuminated me in her light.

Sara Adams, it said.

1958-2009.

Sara was smiling wide, her brown eyes full of laughter.

Not a harsh line on her face.

Not a hint of bitterness or contempt in her smile.

The voices pointed out they'd chosen a photo from before I was born.

"She's probably dead because of you," they said in unison.

I slipped from Sara's light to the darkness backstage, waiting for my eyes to adjust. I contemplated what the voices said and decided they were right. It was true. She was dead because of me.

When my eyes adjusted, my gaze fell on Chuck, who was lurking backstage, half-hidden behind some equipment road cases. He leered at me, just as he had all those years ago.

Pay no attention to the man behind the curtain.

Nobody else ever did.

Sara was dead because of me, and Chuck was back in my life, and for a moment, I wanted him to pump me full of whatever the hell was in that syringe that night. I longed for that synthetic warmth again, if only for a little while. Maybe he'd use too much this time, and I would just fade away.

I walked down the hallway, bypassing the press room, where I was supposed to be in about two minutes. I ignored the concerned glances of passing crew members, found the nearest "Exit" sign, and walked out.

Alice has left the building.

CATCH TWENTY-TWO
—May 7, 2010

Humans are the only creatures on the planet who sense danger and run to it, instead of away. Did you know that? I read that somewhere. I think it's because of our so-called evolved intelligence. We have the ability to rationalize away what our instincts tell us to avoid at all costs. Opposable thumbs and the inability to run from situations that will harm us, that's what we've got.

So, today was the big announcement that *Wonderland* is resuming their tour with me in Sara's place.

The rumor about the tour resuming has been flying around since the Hall of Fame, but today it was made official.

The performance at the Hall of Fame (hereinafter HoF) premiered on HBO last week. I haven't watched it yet, and probably never will, but it's been called a great success in the media.

As one reviewer wrote, "Alice commanded the stage like a veteran maestro, her arm calling up every crescendo of the drums, her foot stomping out her father's bass line. She even managed to keep Alfie where she wanted him, behind her, a feat never before perfected, even by her mother."

I'm not sure what the hell performance that guy was watching. I don't remember any of that, but it made me smile to think about Alfie reading that review.

They're calling us *Wonderland, with Alice Moriarty* instead of just *Wonderland* for this tour. I guess to try and take the sting out of it for Sara's more ardent fans? I'm not sure if they think these people are stupid or what, but I can't imagine tacking on "with Alice Moriarty" will somehow make this okay with them.

Poor Jett has had to deal with all the bullshit with the promoters and the insurers. Of course, the lawyers have been involved too, but Jett's been in it everyday, making sure the band's best interests are protected. I feel bad for him. He looks beat.

I did some math. I don't know the exact numbers, but at an average cost of eighty dollars per concert ticket (and that's a conservative estimate for a reunion tour of this magnitude), multiplied by 18,000 tickets sold per show, that's $1,440,000 that the promoter has to potentially reimburse to fans, per show. *Wonderland* made it through forty of their shows before Sara kicked the bucket. Seventy-two shows remained unfulfilled. That's close to $104,000,000 at stake.

Tickets for the old tour will be honored at the door for the new tour, and returned tickets will be made available for purchase. So, basically, there's a lot riding on the reaction of the fans to this announcement today. If there's a strong backlash and nobody wants to take a chance on me, we'll have to scrap the tour, and the boys could be on the hook for that $104,000,000.

If there's no backlash, or new people buy up the returned tickets, we'll go ahead with the tour, and I'll get to deal with Alfie's bullshit every day for the next six months or so.

That man has been crankier than ever lately, grumbling about how he's being forced to do this tour with me. He's a grown man, though. If he really hated the idea of the tour, he wouldn't do it. He could say no, any of them could, and that would be the end of it. Alfie walked away from *Wonderland* in 1988, and there was nothing any of them could do. The band was done. He could do it again, and that would be that.

However, he's agreed to this tour, despite his insistence he's being forced to, so it stands to reason he doesn't really hate the idea of it. He just likes to act like he does, because stirring up my anxiety gives him great joy.

I don't know what I hope for more: a strong backlash so I don't have to go through with this, but then know, once again, it was me who was responsible for the disbandment of this band, or that the reaction is positive and none of the tickets are returned, or all the returned tickets are bought up, which means I have to spend the next six months literally in the shadow of my dead mother. (They've already decided the backdrop from the HoF would be a part of the stage design for the tour.)

That's the mother of all catch twenty-twos, so to speak. Damned if I do; damned if I don't.

Oh, and because I can't sleep unless I know everything my brain decides it needs to know before it rests, I just did the math on the tour merchandise, too, and, at conservative estimates, each member of the band takes home about $67,000, per night, for the merchandise alone.

That's right. The members of *Wonderland* make more money on tour, per night, on just their cut of merchandise than most people make in a year.

Mull that one over for a while. I'm going to try and get some sleep.

WONDERLAND, WITH ALICE MORIARTY
—May 17, 2010

Six months in the shadow of my dead mother it is!

My only companions? Her cranky ex-boyfriend, my alcoholic father, a hippie drummer and my former stepfather, who seems entirely too exhausted to deal with anybody's bullshit for another five minutes, let alone six months.

The fan reaction to this tour announcement has been positive, somehow, and now that we know people will actually show up, I was told I would need to sign a contract with the promoters. These are the same promoters that very nearly sued us six months ago. Well, very nearly sued them, that is. The boys. A fickle town, this is.

Sara collapsed after the first of what would have been eight shows at the Hollywood Bowl in L.A. Those eight shows would have wrapped up the first part of the U.S. and Canada leg of the tour. They'd have stayed in L.A., gotten some rest, and then headed off for the second leg of the U.S. tour about a month later.

There was great discussion this week (I'm told) about whether or not this tour should pick up where that one left off, with those seven ill-fated Los Angeles dates, or if the remaining dates should be rescheduled as a completely new tour. The schedule revamp won out decidedly. It's very rare that any act would start a tour in Los Angeles. L.A. is where their celebrity peers congregate for entertainment. Most bands prefer to start elsewhere in the country and work out any potential kinks before reaching their buddies in L.A.

With me at the helm, the list of potential kinks is like a mile long. I'd be okay if we just skipped L.A. all together, but I guess that isn't an option.

So, *Wonderland, with Alice Moriarty* will start its new old tour in Columbus, Ohio on Thursday, September 9, 2010, a year to the day that the original Wonderland started its reunion tour. I'm not positive the powers that be are aware of this, but I can't imagine they're not. They will tie Sara to this tour in every way possible, and rightly so, I suppose. Looking at it objectively, this makes sense. Tying Sara to it will keep the fans happy. Keeping the fans happy means more money for everybody (except the fans).

Looking at it the only way I can seem to look at it, highly subjectively, I think it's exploitative as fuck. This whole tour is.

Maybe that's why I agreed to do it.

It's true that there would have been some financial difficulties had we not gone through with this, but, in the end, everybody is going to end up with a fuckton more money than if Sara hadn't died. The merchandise alone has nearly doubled in quantity. Anything you can imagine that they can plant Sara's name and/or face on will be available at the venues: t-shirts, sweatshirts, coffee mugs, tea cups (mad ones, of course) shot glasses, full-sized posters, half-sized posters, playing cards, necklaces, and rings. I think I even saw a snow globe on the list.

If they offered that with cocaine inside as the fake snow, that would be a true homage to Sara.

There will also be merchandise with me on it. That is a very awkward thing for me. I don't know who they think will buy that stuff. And if it does sell, that means my face will be out walking around the streets, or tacked up on someone's walls or crammed in somebody's kitchen cabinets. It's weird.

They're bringing in a photographer next week to take some photos of me for this purpose. *Rolling Stone, People, Variety, The Hollywood Reporter* and *Billboard* have scheduled photographers this week as well.

If any of them suggest I dress up as Alice in Wonderland, I will promptly riot in the streets.

ENOUGH
—May 31, 2010

We had a band meeting last night to discuss some details of the tour. It was the first time I was officially invited to a band meeting. My days of lurking on staircases are at an end!

The meeting was to discuss various issues, including the set list and aforementioned merchandise.

Things got a little heated when Jett brought up the idea of me playing guitar on some songs. That got Alfie up and pacing in a hurry.

"No way," he said.

"Why not?" said Jett.

"Let me guess," I said. "It'd be like spitting on her grave?"

"That's inappropriate, Alice," said Jett.

Over his shoulder, a grin pulled at the corner of Alfie's mouth, and I narrowed my eyes. Stuart snickered but wiped the smile from his face when Jett turned the look on him.

I shoved myself deeper into the couch and chomped into an apple, muttering, "This whole thing is inappropriate."

"You've said yourself a second guitar would add to the sound," said Stuart.

"Not with her playing it," said Alfie.

"What the hell's wrong w-" A piece of apple fell out of my mouth.

"You've grown into such a lady," said Stuart.

"Shut up," I said and then looked at Alfie. "What the hell's wrong with my playing?"

"It took you a month to learn, and I use the term learn here very loosely, seven songs for the Hall of Fame, and that was lyrics only," said Alfie. "It'll take you six months to learn the lyrics and chords to eighteen more. We don't have that kind of time."

It really sucks having the exact insecurities that keep you up at night thrown in your face.

And if I haven't said it in a while: fuck that guy.

(He was right, of course, but still, fuck that guy.)

Jett sighed. "You've agreed to this tour, Alfie. At some point you're just going to have to come to terms with the fact that she's here."

"He hasn't done that in twenty-one years," I muttered.

Alfie drew in a breath and looked to the ceiling. He exhaled and looked at me. "Can I talk?"

I gestured for him to continue with an exaggerated sweep of my arm.

"I have to do this tour," said Alfie. "I don't have to come to terms with a goddamn thing."

"See?" I said to Jett.

"Alice, enough," said Stephen.

Yeah. You read that right. That wasn't Jett. It was Stephen. Scolding me.

Everybody, the four of us, stopped and looked at him.

Well, they looked. I scowled. What was he trying to do, parent me? Much too little, much too late. It sent my bad mood into miserable territory.

"Can I go?" I asked, looking at Jett.

"There are a few more things to discuss," said Jett.

"Do I need to be here for it?" I asked. "Does anybody actually want my input?"

"No," said Alfie.

It was my turn to draw in a deep breath. I kept my eyes on Jett. "Can I go?"

Jett nodded.

I grabbed my bag and ran up the stairs. On the way out of the house, I grabbed Stephen's whiskey bottle from the counter and took it with me. It was almost full. I hope it was his only one.

Now, it's late, too damn late, and I've drank all the whiskey, in case he came looking for it. Ha. Too bad for you, jackass.

The room is spinning. It's spinning bad. All I want to do is lie down, but I know if I do, the spinning will get worse, and then I'll throw up, and I hate throwing up. I hate bathrooms.

How does Stephen do this without getting nauseous? He passes out all the time. I'd like to just pass out without throwing up for hours.

I tried playing my guitar, but my fingers didn't cooperate.

So I've just been wandering the apartment. I put on headphones and listened to music and wandered. I listened to *Wonderland* music. I might as well get a jump on learning these songs before rehearsal. Assuming I'll remember any of this tomorrow.

It's good music. It really is. It's so fucking hard for me to be objective about it. I can't seem to listen to it without thinking about other things. Bad things. Bad things named Chuck and Alfie and Sara. But, really, it is something special. It's no wonder they're up there as one of the greatest rock bands in the world.

And now I'm a part of it. I'm not sure how I feel about that.

I'm tired of wandering. I'm so tired. I'd give anything to be able to fall asleep or pass out or just rest my eyes.

Maybe I'll read.

EXCERPT FROM SARA'S JOURNAL
—June 1, 2010

Entry Date: December 3, 2009:

We've just arrived back in L.A. Three full days off before we start at The Hollywood Bowl.

It's amazing how smoothly things are going. We haven't fought once, not about anything hugely significant. Just little squabbles here and there but that is to be expected. Nobody has thrown the past in anybody's face. Alfie and Stephen are acting like best friends again. It's like old times again, except for the fact that we're all old now.

Every time I look in the mirror, I'm startled by the hag staring back at me. When did that happen? The boys, they've aged beautifully, all of them. Jett included. They take my breath away. Maturity is attractive on men. Men are allowed to age. Women are criticized for it. We aren't allowed to do it.

I keep seeing the same astonishment from fans when I walk out on stage. Astonishment at the hag. They come expecting Sara from twenty years ago and instead they get me. It must be a let down.

Alfie kissed me goodbye after we got off the jet, before we got into our cars. He even opened my car door for me. He's the old Alfie again. It's gone, it seems. His anger. He even asked if I wanted to have dinner with him while we're home. I said yes.

I'm so happy I could burst. I don't know if I trust it. I keep waiting for the other shoe to drop. It always does. The repercussions from the last one went on for two decades. ~SEA

Repercussions.

Is that what we're calling me now?

That was the last entry in her last journal. Those were the last words she ever wrote.

BLUUUUR
—September 23, 2010

It's all a blur. Touring. I didn't expect this. There's absolutely no difference from one day to the next.

That's not true. There's one difference: the city.

Before each show, Jett scrawls the name of the city we're in on the wall backstage at the bottom of the steps. Apparently, Stephen is notorious for forgetting what city they're in and has blurted out the wrong city from time to time.

Put down the whiskey, dude.

You wouldn't think that was a big deal: saying the wrong city, but these people take it seriously. The mere mention of their city's name sends them into a tizzy. And forget it if you say it's the greatest city with the best fans in the world. They get really pumped up then.

Fuck yeah, we're the best!

How many of them have gone to shows in other cities and realized that we say the same thing everywhere?

They say the same thing everywhere, I should say. I don't say much. I just stand at my mic and sing like a good puppy. On occasion, I'll wander back to Stuart's kit, and we goof off with each other, mainly when the other two are talking to the crowd. We're like naughty children on a car ride with mom, dad and 18,000 of their friends.

Other than the city, it's all the same. I thought touring would be more exciting. Mostly, it's just exhausting—dragging my ass from one plane to the next or one hotel to the next or one arena to the next. Sightseeing might help, but I'm too fucking tired for that.

I get up. I eat. I get on the phone and do some interviews and then answer emails. I scour the web for any mention of my name and then obsess about every comment made by journalists and total strangers. Some of them are nice. Many are not. Some are just outrageous with their theories and ideas about our situation as a band.

Basically, if I act like Sara, they say I'm trying too hard to be her, but if I'm just myself, they say I'm trying too hard not to be her. If Alfie is friendly with me on stage or vice versa, they say we're clearly having an affair. If we're cold to each other, they say we're locked in a lover's quarrel. If Stephen and Alfie get along, they say the best friends have finally found their way back to each other now that Sara has died, and if they don't get along, they say Stephen has finally discovered that Alfie is my bio dad, and now those two are engaged in another bitter feud.

The only one who seems to come out unscathed by these people is Stuart. What's his trick?

I've also decided that, by the end of this tour, if not before then, I will end up more traumatized by Stephen being my father than by Sara being my mother.

I wandered out of my room a few minutes ago, in search of vending machine sustenance. These hotels are too fancy for my tastes. I don't recognize half the food on the room service menu, and the prices are so ridiculous for the things I might consider eating there's no way I'd order any of it. $165 for a cheeseburger! That doesn't include the fries. And even if I wanted to spend that kind of money on a fucking cheeseburger, I wouldn't because these burgers have things like duck eggs and truffles and caviar on them.

Yick.

Anyway, halfway between my room and my snack oasis, a room door opened and out popped a groupie. She was easy to identify as such. They all look the same: vapid, leggy, young. This one wore heels so high she moved like a fawn who'd wandered away from its mother—a drunken fawn in a crop top and mini-skirt. She couldn't have been any older than me. In a parallel universe (a long, long way away) we might even have been friends.

I stopped. She stopped. We stared at each other.

"Oh my god, you're Alice!" she squealed, throwing her arms around me. "It's so nice to meet you!"

Behind her, my father appeared, naked but for his underwear. Boxers, thank god. This was the point when I decided I wasn't hungry anymore.

Still caught in Bambi's vice grip, arms pinned to my sides, I said to him over her shoulder, "Really?"

He scratched the back of his head sheepishly and shrugged.

"Do you know where my friends are?" she squeaked at Stephen, releasing me.

If her friends had appeared from behind Stephen, I swear I would have launched myself out of the nearest window, Diary.

Stephen shook his head. "Sorry, love. I only had eyes for you tonight."

Ugh.

She giggled, of course. "Oh, well. I'm sure they're fine."

No grown woman should sound like that. She sounded like a Valley Girl on helium, which is strange because I think we're in Minnesota.

"I had fun," she said. "Thanks."

"Me too, baby." He kissed her cheek. "Get home safe."

UGGGH.

She teetered off for the elevator. I forced the bile back into my stomach and went back to my room. Now I'm sitting here trying to erase all of it from my memory, but some things just cannot be unseen.

KNOCK KNOCK
—September 29, 2010

It's very hard sometimes, being up there. I hate knowing everybody wishes it was her and not me, including those who share the stage with me.

There are points during every show when Alfie and I kind of turn to each other and sing. It's perfunctory; just a part of the show. It plays to those dirty little minds in the crowd who lust for me and him to be together. That is an unsettling and rapidly growing craze, by the way.

Those moments are just two singers playing off each other. There's no real passion behind them. It's acting. When he looks at me during those times, he sees me.

There are other times when he's lost in his performance, and he looks to his left, and I know he sees her. I know it. At least for a few seconds. In those moments, he's the Alfie from those pictures I found at Sara's house, the young man untouched by bitterness and time and success. I know it will only be a second before he remembers it's me. He'll blink and his face will fall. He'll blink again, and he'll be back to perfunctory Alfie.

Those blinks are crushing. I know I say I hate him, and I probably do, but I don't wish the pain I see in those eyes on anybody. He loses her again and again, night after night.

Because of me.

They see her too, the audience. They see whatever part of her lives in me, I think. They see a "Sara in Wonderland" they were denied all those years.

Because of me.

Nobody sees me.

As one reviewer put it, "Alice is a haunting reminder of what music lost when Sara died."

I had to get out of my room. These thoughts were driving me crazy. So, I went down to the hotel bar and pulled up a stool.

Stuart wandered into the hotel not long after, with the night's conquest on his arm. This one was an unsteady, toothpick blond in a delicate state of sobriety.

He spotted me and whispered something to her, soon setting out across the lobby on his way to me. It took him a full five minutes to make the thirty meter walk because of requests for pictures and autographs from fans. That would drive me insane. Stuart handled it like a gentleman though; as gentlemanly as he could be with a drunken sorority woman-child waiting in the wings.

"Hey, Little One," he said.

"Don't call me that," I said.

He held up his hands defensively and gestured to the bartender, settling onto the barstool beside me. The bartender poured him a drink and set it in front of him.

"Want to talk about it?" he asked.

"No," I said.

He nodded.

"You knew her well, right?" I asked.

"Who?"

"Sara."

"Oh. Well, I didn't know her as well as the other three," he said, making a crude sexual gesture with his finger and fist.

I laughed. He leaned into me with his shoulder.

"I knew her well enough," he said. "Why?

"What was she like before I was born?" I asked. "The truth."

He hesitated, and I thought he meant to lie, to spare my feelings, but then shrugged. "Happier."

I nodded. It was no surprise.

"But a lot of shit went down right before you were born," he said.

"Shit that was a direct result of her getting pregnant," I said.

He shook his head. "No, not all of it." He considered. "Well, yeah, pretty much all of it."

I nodded. "No wonder she hated me."

"She didn't hate you."

"She didn't like me very much," I said, kicking back my drink.

I could feel him watching me. "You know, I remember this one time when I was at your house. You were very young still. Jett had hollered at you for tracking dirt into the house, and you were on the verge of tears. Sara grabbed your hand and took you back outside with her. She grabbed handfuls of dirt and told you to do the same, and you guys brought them inside."

I looked at him, my curiosity piqued.

"Sara jammed her tongue out at Jett and danced around, throwing the dirt into the air as he swept up the original mess, and so did you," said Stuart "You two had a blast. Even Jett didn't stay mad long."

"You made that up," I said.

"I did not!"

"Why don't I remember any of it?"

"You were like four," said Stuart.

"I still think I would remember something about it," I said.

He shrugged. "It's the truth. I swear it. Ask Jett if you don't believe me."

"Maybe I will."

"I mean, she was definitely drunk or high or both at the time," said Stuart. "But you did have a good time together that day."

Stuart's story did not jive at all with the Sara I remembered, but I suppose he was right about the age thing.

I remembered something and turned around. Stuart's groupie was pacing the lobby, her nose stuck down in her phone.

"Your play thing is getting bored," I said.

Stuart turned too, leaning back against the bar. We watched her together.

"I forgot about her," he said.

"That's a shame," I said. "I thought for sure it was true love."

Stuart's eyes drifted to me, narrowed. "It might do you a bit of good to find a play thing of your own."

I gestured for another drink. "I don't play well with others."

"You haven't even tried," he said. He leaned in closer, his smile devilish. "If you want, I could ditch the blond and..."

"Oh, gross," I said. "You've known me since I was born, you pervert."

Stuart shrugged, not bothered in the slightest.

"Plus, you're like a hundred."

"Oh, fuck off."

I laughed, holding up my drink to him. "Go wrangle up that poor girl before she wanders off on her own. It's a scary world out there for a child."

"She's not that young."

"She's younger than me."

"Debatable," said Stuart.

"Not that that matters to you, apparently," I said.

"You should see the one your dad snagged," he said.

I groaned. "No, thank you. I met the one he got the other night, and that was plenty for me."

"Minnesota?"

"Yeah. Nice girl. Sweet," I said. "Hopefully out of high school."

Stuart chuckled.

"Do you guys check IDs?"

"Shut up."

I smiled and a thought passed through my mind. "What'd Alfie get?"

Stuart waved his hand. "Oh, Alfie's not the groupie sort."

I looked at him, eyebrows raised.

"He never was," he said. "My guess is, he's up in his room right now, snuggling one of his guitars."

Stuart left to attend to his young friend, and I contemplated what he'd said.

I just couldn't believe that Alfie wasn't into groupies. He was gorgeous, and rich, and considered one of the greatest musicians in modern history.

Beautiful women threw themselves at him wherever he went. How was it possible that he didn't indulge in them?

So, I went to his room to check it out. Alfie answered the door wearing plaid pajama bottoms, a white tee shirt, and reading glasses perched on his nose. Sure enough, there were no signs of groupies anywhere.

Hmm.

He sighed and leaned against the door when he saw it was me.

"Can I come in?" I asked.

He hesitated but then walked back into the room. I took that as consent to follow him and stopped the door before it slammed in my face.

The floor was scattered with pieces of paper. He sat cross-legged on the floor and started to play his guitar, stopping every few moments to jot something down on the papers. I sat in the chair adjacent to him and watched.

"Am I interrupting?" I asked.

"Yes," he said, almost too quickly.

"Do you want me to go?"

"Do whatever you want," he said after a moment.

He started to play a beautiful tune.

"Is that something new?"

"Have you heard it before?" he said.

"No."

"Then it's new, isn't it?"

I thought to get upset then, but he looked at me over the rim of his glasses, and there was a twinkle in his eyes that suggested he was only teasing, so I settled down.

He continued to regard me closely, still playing.

"What?" I said.

"You look like shit."

I laughed. "Gee, thanks."

"Not sleeping?"

"Not well."

He nodded. After a moment, the song changed to "Little One." When I realized what it was, I smiled.

"Is that really about me?" I asked.

He looked at me again but didn't respond.

"I'll deny it if asked, but I've always loved it," I said.

He smiled and went back to the original song.

I dug through my bag and pulled out the stack of photos from Sara's nightstand, the photos of her and Alfie that he'd sent her before the reunion tour started. I turned them over in my hands several times and then tossed them on the floor in front of him.

He stopped playing and cocked his head to look at them.

"I found them at Sara's place," I said. "I thought maybe you'd want them back."

He set the guitar aside and picked them up. He rifled through a few of them and then his shoulders slumped, and his chin dropped to his chest. He didn't say anything, or even move.

"I didn't mean to upset you," I said.

He laughed. "Oh, sure you did. But I deserve it, don't I?"

He hopped to his feet and wiped his wet eyes with the back of his hand. He refilled his drink and poured one for me.

I watched him play for a while.

"Can I ask you something without you getting pissed off?" I said.

He half-laughed, half-scoffed. "Let's say yes."

"You loved her," I said.

"That's your question?"

"Why didn't you ever come back to her?" I said. "It's all she ever wanted."

He stopped playing. "That question doesn't have a simple answer, Alice."

"It was because of me, right?" I said.

He looked at me.

"I'm sorry," I said.

"Sorry for what? Existing?" he asked. "That's a stupid thing to be sorry for."

His mini-outburst surprised me and not because he wasn't prone to outbursts, but because it sounded more compassionate than angry.

"Never apologize to me again for existing," he said. "Okay?"

In a way, it felt like I'd waited my whole life to hear him say that, but it didn't bring me any relief. Hearing it didn't make me feel any less lost. If anything, I was just more confused.

"I think maybe you're the only one who ever really knew her," I said. "The only one she ever let see the real her."

He watched me.

"I wonder what that was like," I said.

He had no answer for me, and I didn't expect one. He picked up his guitar and started playing. I finished my drink and left.

FOUND IT IN A BAR?
—September 29 or 30, 2010

I don't know what the hell happened.

I really don't.

I left the hotel after I left Alfie's room.

I wound up in some seedy bar somewhere in the city. I don't even know what city.

What the hell city are we in?

The place reminded me of The Hole. It felt comfortable, so I drank. I guess I drank a lot. I don't remember much.

At some point, I found myself back on the street, heading back to the hotel. There were photographers everywhere. They seemed to come out of nowhere. They swarmed me, just like the night Sara died. I was blinded by the camera flashes again, just like that night.

I made it back to the hotel, somehow, and they followed me in. I don't think that was allowed. They followed me through the front doors and wouldn't leave me alone. They just kept taking pictures, hundreds of them. How many fucking photos do they need?

I lashed out at them finally, shoving at them, swinging at them. "Fucking vultures."

I ended up spread-eagle on the floor.

Jett appeared, cell phone in hand, and he helped me up, shielding me from them. The doorman, the concierge and the manager headed off the vultures while Jett led me to the elevators.

I leaned on him as we waited for the car to arrive.

"You can't just walk out like that anymore, Alice," he said, arm around me.

I shrugged and leaned most of my weight on him. "I needed some fresh air."

"Found it in a bar, did you?" he said.

He used the tone he used with Stephen when Stephen was drunk. It made me cranky.

I pushed away from him as the car arrived, walking onto the elevator by myself. He followed. I leaned against the railing on one side and stared at him across the elevator. I felt very angry.

He studied my face, his eyes full of concern and confusion. "Alice, what is it?"

"Nothing," I said. My eyelids felt heavy.

"Something," he said. "It looks like you have something to say."

I thought about Chuck then, and how nobody had ever even asked me why I'd tried to kill myself. Nobody had anything to say about that. Not that night or any night since. Not even Jett.

"What could I possibly have to say, Jett?" I asked.

The "ding" of the elevator signaled our arrival on our floor. He tried to help me out, but I wouldn't let him. I tried to slide the key into my door and missed. Jett tried to help, but I wouldn't let him. After several more clumsy attempts, he stepped in and took the card from me and unlocked the door.

"Alice, please talk to me," he said.

I stepped inside and closed the door in his face.

I can't sleep now. The room is spinning again. I want to lie down, but I don't want to throw up.

And I don't remember what happened between getting to the bar and leaving it, but there's a baggie of what I think is cocaine in my bag.

I took it out when I got back and set it on the pillow.

I stared at it for a long time.

I'm still staring at it now.

It's all I can see.

YOU'RE NOT HER
—September 30, 2010

Well, I finally fell asleep about dawn last night. This morning. Whatever. I could have slept straight through the day and night, but there was a show to do. There's no calling in sick with this stuff. You can call in dead, but not sick.

The pictures of me from last night are everywhere; all over the web. They're awful. I look awful. My face is red and puffy. My eyes look dead. It's horrific. I really could've just crawled into a cave for a very long time.

But, instead, I had to go sing in front of 18,000 people. Just as good, right?

A flood of fans were waiting for us when we arrived at the arena.

Oh, we're in Vegas, by the way. Apparently, all the bright lights and massive casinos didn't register with me last night. That explains the plethora of photographers. Vegas is crawling with them. They're generally more polite than they are in, say, L.A. They're not allowed in many of the resorts, but if somebody famous goes wandering the streets alone and gets hammered, they'll find her.

And now I'm famous, whatever the hell that means—I'm the exact same person I was before this fucking tour, and nobody gave a shit about me then—so I should probably stop wandering the streets alone.

Just like Jett said.

I hate it when he's right.

The Vegas show was the first time I was bombarded with requests for autographs as we walked into the arena. I have those pictures to thank, I guess. I've drummed up some bad-girl, rock-star mystique for myself, it seems.

It was mostly young girls who asked for the autographs too. Not the groupie types, but normal girls. Normal girls looking to...what? Be like me? Hey, kids. Drink your way into infamy!

Many of them wanted photos with me and Alfie together. I heard someone ask Alfie what he thought of all the attention I was getting. I could feel his eyes on me after that, as we signed more autographs. I sensed the exact moment something crawled up his ass about me, because his brooding is like an energy field. You can't see it, but when you're caught in it you're definitely aware that something is amiss.

By show time, any trace of kindness he'd shown to me or minuscule feeling of endearment he might have developed for me had disappeared. I swear to God, he screwed up some of his chords during the show so it sounded to the audience like my voice was off key. I was too exhausted to care, let alone retaliate.

At the end of the show, fans in and near the front row threw teddy bears and flowers on the stage. I thought they were for Alfie or maybe Stephen, although they generally get classier gifts thrown at them, like underwear and bras. One of the bears smacked me in the head. The fans cheered when I picked it up, and I realized it was for me, and so were the flowers.

It was pretty cool; ridiculous, but pretty cool. I was actually feeling pretty good by the time I headed offstage.

But my energy disappeared once the lights and the sounds of stage were gone. I felt like I couldn't take one more step, or even stand. I had absolutely nothing left.

"Fuck," I said, slumping on to the couch in my dressing room, putting my face in my hands.

I remembered the coke then. It was a bad idea, of course. A very bad idea. I still had no idea where I'd gotten it or if it was actually even cocaine. And, let's face it, the last time I'd done coke it hadn't turned out so well. But I felt I wouldn't even have made it to the plane without some sort of pick me up.

I pulled the powder out of my bag and stared at it. I dipped my finger in it and touched it to my tongue. It numbed on contact.

Definitely cocaine.

I stared at it another couple seconds and then sprinkled some on to the table. I found a dollar bill and rolled it, and, like a good little rock star, I snorted the powder.

I flipped my head back, sniffing in again.

A flash of memory from long ago invaded my mind. It was of Chuck doing the same as I had just done, and then holding the drug out for me.

Want some?

It burned as much as it did the first time.

The door flew open and Alfie stormed into the room. Startled, I popped up and shoved the coke in my bag.

I waited for him to say something, but he just stood there. His chest rose and fell visibly, and his fists were clenched at his sides. It looked as if the Mad Hatter had caught a bit of what ailed The Hulk.

"What?" I asked.

He moved too quickly for me to react and the next moment he had me pinned against the wall, one hand around my neck. I fought him, but he trapped me to the wall with his body.

"You're not her," he said. His lips were against my cheek because I'd turned my face away from him. The whiskey on his breath was unmistakable. "You hear that? You're *not* her."

Like I needed anybody else to fucking tell me that? Especially him.

"You're right," I said, turning my face to him. Our faces were only an inch apart. "I'm alive."

He growled and squeezed my neck tighter before releasing me.

As soon as he let go, I shoved him away from me. He tried to retaliate, but I knocked his hands away. Fuck that. I pushed him again. You come at me, I'm coming at you, asshole. For the first time in years, I was feeling pretty damn good about myself, and he ruined it.

Even through my anger, though, despite the fact that he had just attacked me, it was hard for me to deny my attraction to him. That pissed me off even more.

"Alive and well," I said.

I pushed him up against the door and crushed my lips to his, putting my hands under his shirt. He resisted at first but slowly returned the kiss. It reminded me of the kiss that day with Chuck in the Great Room six years earlier, and I wondered what my life would have been like if I had been brave enough to grab one of those knives and stab him to death with it.

When we broke for air, Alfie's expression was a pretty good mix of surprise and...desire?

Hmm.

But I was too angry to think too much about desire.

I dug my nails into his skin and dragged them down his torso. He drew in a quick, pained breath and heaved me away. I nearly lost my balance but regained my footing soon enough.

"I'm not weak like her either," I said, stepping to him again. "You put your hands on me like that again, and I'll kill you."

I turned away, disgusted; disgusted with him, disgusted with myself. It was all disgusting. My entire life was disgusting.

I looked for something to take the edge off—the edge off the effects of the cocaine, which I'd snorted to take the edge off the exhaustion.

Vicious cycle.

"She wasn't weak until you came along," said Alfie, and his voice was so low it was almost a whisper.

I rounded on him, eyes wide. My heart hammered at my ribcage and a bead of sweat formed at my brow.

"Get out," I said.

He didn't.

"Goddammit!" I grabbed something from the table—an ashtray maybe—and hurled it at him. He ducked at the last second. It struck the door behind him and left an indentation. "Get out!"

He left.

It wasn't thirty seconds later that Jett came in. I really need to start locking my door.

"What was Alfie doing in here?" he asked.

I laughed. It was funny. At least, it was then. Right now, I can't really remember why.

Jett watched me, eyebrows furrowed. He noticed the ashtray by his foot and then the damaged door behind him. His eyes drifted to me, and then to the table, and he spotted the white residue.

Busted.

"Where is it?" he asked.

"Where is what?"

He crossed the room and grabbed my bag, dumping it out on the couch. Of course, the coke was right on top and fell out first. He held the baggie up.

"This shit again?" he asked.

This shit again.

He was acting like I'd been a habitual user or something. Christ. I'd only ever done the stuff once before in my life.

Jett walked into the bathroom, and I heard the toilet flush. He returned with the empty baggie and threw it in the trash.

"Oh, nice," I said. "Do you know how much that cost me?"

It would have been nice if he knew the answer to that, actually, because I didn't.

"Your life, nearly," said Jett. "If I recall correctly."

I rolled my eyes. "Now who's got a flair for the melodramatic?"

"We can get you help," he said.

"I don't need help."

"Oh, sure!" he said, throwing up his hands. "You can stop any time you want, right? You're getting to be more like your father everyday!"

I lost it. I pushed him. I can't believe I pushed Jett, but cocaine will do that to you. I pushed him again, and he was so unprepared for it he nearly fell over.

I grabbed the front of his jacket. "Maybe it wasn't the drugs, Jett. Did you ever think of that? Maybe it wasn't the drugs that made me want to kill myself that night!"

He looked stunned. "Alice, I..."

"Just get out," I said, letting go of him.

I never thought I'd be saying that to Jett. Not ever.

He reached for me, but I stepped away from him. I had nothing left to throw, so I just shouted this time.

"Get out!"

He did.

I sat on the couch and cried.

DADDY ISSUES
—October 1, 2010

We have five days off. Thank fuck. I flew home after Vegas, and I flew commercial so I didn't have to deal with any of them.

Jett's been calling non-stop, of course, but I don't want to talk to him. I guess it's nice to know he cares though. Stephen probably didn't even notice I wasn't on the band's plane, and Alfie probably hoped they left me in Vegas forever.

You'd think I would've just gone to my place when I got home, but, as has been well-established by now, I am not the best decision-maker, and instead I wound up at Sara's house.

I wandered the house, just like I did when I went there after she died. I can't seem to stop doing that. I don't know what the hell I'm hoping to find. It hasn't revealed itself in twenty-one years. It probably never will.

I ended up in her media room and rifled through the drawers and shelves in it. I came across a stack of old VHS tapes tucked in the back of one of the shelves. Their faded labels told me they had something to do with *Wonderland*.

Now, it's not hard to find videos of *Wonderland* performances if you're feeling inclined to watch them. They're all over the Internet. There is a slue of high-quality videos out there from their reunion tour, recorded by concert-goers in the crowd. I suspect many of those people are now earning a pretty penny selling them on DVD. Those who recorded their very last show before Sara died could be millionaires by now, but maybe that was just my cynical side talking.

These tapes were different though; they were old, for one. Obviously. They were fucking VHS tapes. I remembered reading somewhere, or maybe it was Jett who told me, that *Wonderland* had a videographer on the road with them back in the day. My superior investigative instincts told me that these were some of those tapes.

I found a VCR buried at the bottom of a stack of more technologically-advanced media equipment in a cabinet in the wall, and slid one of the tapes in. It took five more minutes to find the right input selection on the damn television, but then Sara was on the screen.

She was very young, and she was standing at a mirror in what looked like a room backstage, fussing with her hair. Alfie came into the picture and put an arm around her shoulders, whispering something in her ear. They both giggled.

"Ah, your Highnesses," said Stephen from behind the camera.

Alfie and Sara turned as one. Alfie bowed to the camera and Sara curtsied.

"This here is—what was it they called you?" The camera bobbed around a little and Stephen called out. "What was it?"

Stuart's voice came from somewhere behind the camera, but it was muffled.

"What?" said Stephen, swinging the camera around to Stuart.

"The prince and princess of rock and roll," said Stuart, rifling through an issue of *Rolling Stone*. He found the page he was searching for and began to read from it. "Sara, a poetic, raven-haired beauty, and Alfie, a striking front man and brooding, musical genius..." Stuart paused to giggle.

"Shut up," said Alfie from off screen. An object flew through the air, a comb maybe, but Stuart knocked it away before it hit him.

Stuart composed himself and cleared his throat. "...a brooding, musical genius, are the reigning prince and princess of rock and roll."

The camera panned back to Alfie. "You are striking, Alfred," said Stephen. "Incredibly dreamy."

Alfie flipped the camera off, and it was hard not to notice Alfie's discomfort with the accolades about his physical good looks. It occurred to me then that, outside the rock god thing, Alfie was a shy man.

"Ooh, so brooding, too," said Stephen.

"Jealously is very ugly," said Alfie.

Stephen feigned insult. "Bassists get no love, man!"

"Tell that to the hoard of whores waiting for you outside the doors every night," said Sara as she brushed powder over her face.

Alfie and Stuart "ooohed" and snickered.

"Sara Elizabeth, this is a family show!" said Stephen.

He turned the camera around to his face. "Stay away from the whores, children."

The footage must have been from one of their first tours, if not the very first one. If it was the first one, Stephen would have been no older than I was. It was a shock to see him so young and fresh. Clearly, he was under the influence of something. Several things, I would bet, but, despite this, he looked...well. Healthy. And it was the first I'd really seen myself in him, beyond our eyes. I could see myself in his cheeks and nose and smile, too.

I felt an overwhelming sense of appreciation that that footage existed, because the young man in it no longer did, and never had in my lifetime.

"Might I remind you that there is a lovely, little whore in your dressing room at this very moment?" said Stuart, off camera.

Alfie poked his head into frame. "Do as Daddy says not as he does, children."

"Five minutes!" said Jett.

"Shit!" said Sara.

Stephen readjusted the camera and pointed it at Jett, who had poked his head into the room. He was so young! And beautiful. Jett is a beautiful man, but he was downright breathtaking back then. I wondered briefly how many whores had gone after him over the years and if he'd welcomed them or chased them away.

He had that same I'm-too-old-for-this-shit demeanor though.

"Say hello, Jett," said Stephen.

"Hello, Jett," said Jett, and then he was gone.

The camera panned back to Sara and Alfie. Sara shoved Alfie at the camera. "Go away. I have to finish getting beautiful."

Alfie teetered a moment but returned to her, his arm around her neck. "You're always beautiful, baby."

Stephen and Stuart mocked him.

"Gag me, seriously," said Sara.

When Alfie tried to kiss her, she shoved his face away. But then she yanked him back to her for a passionate kiss, before shoving him away again.

Alfie turned to the camera with a grin on his face; the dopey grin of a man in love.

"C'mon," he said, gesturing at Stephen. "Let's go do some stuff we can't show on camera."

The footage ended and the screen went blank.

I sat back and stared at the blank screen, contemplating the realization that my parents weren't always irresponsible fuck-ups.

Well, no, they were exactly that; they were absolutely irresponsible fuck-ups, but they were rock stars and that's what they were supposed to be. It's what they were paid to be. It was only my arrival on the scene that made that unacceptable, and it was only unacceptable to me. Who the fuck was I, really, compared to millions of fans? Nobody.

I think it was about that point I started drinking, and I was drinking straight from the bottle.

I found another tape labeled, "Wonderland's Last Show" and put it in the VCR. It was from 1988. The tape started up during their encore song, the last song they would play together for two decades. The footage was shot from the stage, probably by the aforementioned videographer.

At the end of the song, after they bowed, Sara approached her microphone again. Alfie lingered in the back, as if he was waiting for her.

"I just want you to know, you, my fans, you mean everything to me," said Sara. Her eyes filled with tears. She put a hand on her midsection "You are my world.

You're the reason I do this. You are my great loves. You are my children. I hope you know how much I love you all. Goodnight."

Her adoring fans screamed and clapped and cried and threw flowers at her. It brought tears to my eyes, to be honest. Lots of things bring tears to my eyes when I'm drinking, and of course, by then, I had had...quite a bit.

Sara scooped up as many of the flowers as she could and walked off stage. Alfie followed close behind. The cameraman followed.

It was only seconds later when the fight happened. THE fight; The Fight Heard 'Round The World; the fight that tore Alfie away from Sara and the band for over twenty years, courtesy of little fetus me.

There wasn't much of it to see. The footage was grainy, and the camera was shaky. It captured Sara on the floor at the bottom of the stairs and Alfie standing beside her. There was some shouting, lots of cursing, and Stephen barreled down the steps. I assume whoever shot the video dropped the camera then, to step in and help break up the fight, or maybe Stephen knocked it loose as he'd blown by, because the video ended there.

The security intercom buzzed and scared the shit out of me. I walked to the foyer and looked at the video screen. The footage was as grainy as the video I'd just watched, but there was no denying who was standing just outside the security gate of the property: Alfie.

I sighed, and waited a moment, before pressing the intercom button. "What do you want?"

He jumped and looked around a moment, finding the speaker for the intercom on the wall beside him. He pressed the button.

"How do you know it's me?" he said.

"You're on candid camera," I said.

He looked around again. "Oh."

"Smile," I said.

Despite himself, he laughed, which made me smile.

"Can I—can I come in?" he said.

I watched him and considered. He was still looking around, trying to find the camera, when I pressed the "open sesame" button, and the gate swung open. I opened the front door and waited. Moments later, he was there, and we were facing off over a threshold, yet again.

I stepped aside and gestured him in. It was very weird, watching him walk around the foyer, just like he had that first night I saw him all those years ago. It was almost like watching a video of it that night but from a different vantage point.

"Want something to drink?" I asked, hoisting up my bottle.

"Uh, no," he said. "No, thanks. I won't stay long. I just..." He hesitated. "I guess I just wanted to apologize for the other night."

Holy shit.

Call the papers! This one deserves its own headline.

"Alfie Evans Apologizes to Alice Moriarty."

"What exactly are you apologizing for?" I asked. "Assaulting me or for insinuating my mother is dead because of me?"

He cringed. "Both?"

I sighed, again, and thought it was a good thing he was so good-looking, something I became more and more aware of the more I drank.

I headed back to the media room and flopped down on the couch. He trailed behind and sat beside me hesitantly.

"What's that?" he asked, pointing to the TV.

"A television," I said.

He sighed. "Yes, thank you. What are you watching?"

I rewound the video and pressed play, watching him watch it.

"Oh," he said after a full minute.

It was clear to me that he was still affected by what had happened that night. He swallowed several times and stopped blinking completely. When the video ended, he took the remote from me and rewound it. He paused the video just as he and Sara left stage.

"We hadn't spoken in months," he said, gesturing to the television. "Your mother and me."

The mood in the room turned confessional. I recalled the loving couple I'd watched on video earlier and became curious. Actually, I'd been curious about it my whole life; what had happened between the two of them; how Sara had ended up with Stephen.

"Why weren't you speaking?" I asked.

He continued as if he hadn't heard me. "We had separate everything by then. Separate cars, separate rooms, separate fucking airplanes, for Christ's sake. Separate. We walked onstage together, we sang together, we walked offstage together, but at the bottom of the stairs, we separated and didn't see each other again until the next show."

"Why weren't you speaking?" I asked again.

He shifted forward and put his elbows on his knees.

"I'd asked her to marry me," he said.

Oh.

"Oh," I said. "When?"

"About six months before that night," he said, gesturing to the television again.

"I assume it didn't go well?"

"Why do you say that?" he asked, looking at me.

I grabbed his hand and held it up, tapping his empty ring finger.

"Oh. Yeah. No, it didn't go well at all. She said no. Unequivocally. Just no. She said she didn't want anything to get in the way of our careers, and then I suggested we quit the band and not let our careers get in the way of our relationship. She laughed in my face," he said. "I, uh, I reacted badly."

I feigned disbelief. "No, you?"

He looked at me again, and his lips pulled into a small smile. The smile faded quickly though.

"We fought. I was hurt and angry. She was defensive and angry. I said some things I shouldn't have."

"Is that when she hooked up with Stephen?"

Alfie sighed and bowed his head.

"I left our room after we fought," he said. "I felt ashamed right away for what I'd said to her but couldn't make myself go back inside to apologize. So I just stayed out in the hallway. I could hear her crying through the door..."

He drew in a disjointed breath, and I resisted the urge to put my arms around him. I don't know if it was the alcohol or the fact that he looked so sad, but I felt a strong desire to comfort him.

I felt a strong desire to do other things to him too, and I'm certain that was the alcohol's fault. My wavering attraction to Alfie seemed to be in direct correlation with the amount of booze in my blood stream.

"What'd you say to her?" I asked, mentally pushing aside some less than pure thoughts.

"Oh, something along the lines of 'I hope the band keeps you warm at night' and 'One day soon I'll be gone and you'll have nothing' and that 'Once I'm gone you'll just curl into a pathetic, little ball and die.' Something like that."

"Jesus," I said. "If no one's ever told you, you've got a real way with words."

He chuckled, but there was no humor in it. "It gets worse."

Doesn't it always?

He continued. "The door flew open and Sara came at me. She leaped onto my back and swung at me and scratched me." He looked at me. "Attacking me is kind of like a family tradition for you guys..."

I laughed. I couldn't help it.

"Anyhow, she screamed at me that I was the pathetic one, and that I'd never last a day without her. Jett came out of his room and tried to break us apart. He got her off of me, but she kept hitting me. I turned and shoved at her. I just wanted her away from me..." His voice broke. He bowed his head again. "I didn't realize how close to the stairs we were. She lost her balance and fell down them."

"Holy shit," I said.

"I thought she was dead. She didn't move once she stopped rolling," he said. "But then she started screaming. This gut-wrenching scream."

Alfie swallowed roughly. "I froze. I couldn't move, not even to help her. Jett rushed down the stairs to her. She curled into a ball and was grasping her midsection."

He touched his stomach. "Jett said the doctor told her she'd probably been about two months along."

It took me a minute to understand. "She was pregnant?"

He nodded.

"With your child?" I asked.

He nodded, again. "Mmm hmm."

"Holy shit." I stood and paced and turned back to him. "Did you know?"

"Neither did she," he said, shaking his head. "I was too ashamed of what I'd done to be there for her afterward. I didn't even go to the hospital. I think a part of me has been frozen at the top of those stairs since that night."

I sat back down. Everything was starting to make sense.

"Stephen stepped in to comfort her when I wouldn't, like the helpful friend he is," said Alfie, his voice dripping with barely concealed contempt. "Jett said the doctors told her she'd likely never get pregnant again. The damage was too extensive." He gestured vaguely at me. "Obviously, they were wrong."

He rewound the video again to the point Stephen rushed by the camera and paused it.

"Stephen attacked me this night because he was protecting you and your mother. He thought I'd done it again. He thought I'd found out about you, and that I'd thrown her down the fucking stairs because of it," said Alfie. "But she tripped. She just fucking tripped."

So many pieces of the puzzle were falling into place.

Alfie sat back. "I never even knew she was pregnant, but from the night we lost our baby, I've wondered what our kid would have been like." I felt his eyes on me. "What she would have looked like."

I looked at him. "She?"

"She's always been a she in my mind."

Talk about awkward. Him looking at the kid he wished was his and his best friend's eyes looking back at him. Me staring at the guy who wished I was his kid, unable to ignore how attractive I found him to be.

I looked away and contemplated what he'd just told me.

"So it *was* because of me," I said. "You never came back to her because of me."

It was silent for a second, but then he scoffed. "That's what you got out of that story?"

I looked at him again, and his face had clouded over. Uh oh. Sad, sexy Alfie was gone, and angry, brooding Alfie was back.

"What?" I asked.

He shook his head. "Christ, I knew I shouldn't have come here."

He stood and paced, and I watched him, wondering if he'd ever been to that house without muttering those words.

He turned back to me. "You know, Alice, this might be a hard thing for you to comprehend, but not every fucking thing is about you."

He stormed out.

Now I'm sitting here alone in the wake of Hurricane Evans.

The silence is deafening.

—October 2, 2010

Alice,

My heart is broken.

It's the worst day of my life come back again.

Again, I'm at your bedside holding your limp hand. Again, you are lost to me and to the world. This time, I hear them say you may not return.

Alice, you were created in chaos. The day you were born, the moment your eyes opened and your tiny fingers grasped mine, I swore to a god I don't believe in that I'd never let you let go. I pray to him again now to allow you to wake up.

I'm writing to you in this diary. It's all I can think to do. I've read it too, your diary. I know now exactly what happened to you.

You've kept so much inside, Alice. You've battled it alone, and I don't think I'll ever forgive myself. I'd gladly exchange my life for yours, if only you'd wake up.

Please open your eyes, Alice.

Love,
Jett

PART THREE:
THE END

DESTRUCTION
—October 5, 2010

I'm baaack.

Did you miss me?

Where to begin?

First things first: I see Jett got his hands on this diary. I'm going to have to talk to him about that and about what he wrote. He seems to be feeling very guilty, and he has no reason to feel that way.

I'm also going to have to call him out on his melodramatics. I learned from the best, it seems.

I'll bet you're completely confused right now. I am, too! So, let me tell you what I remember, although I'm not sure how much that will help. The whole thing is pretty foggy still. Well, smoky. It's all pretty smoky still.

After Alfie stormed out of Sara's house, I refreshed my bottle and turned on the TV to quiet the silence. I came across one of those useless, fucking tabloid shows where people have nothing better to do than chatter about famous people, so, of course, I watched to catch up on the latest on *Wonderland*.

About a half hour in, my photo popped up on the screen along side a photo of Chuck Wall, and the conversation became a debate on whether or not Chuck Wall was my mystery rapist.

I panicked.

From what they were saying, I figured out that somebody at Second Fucking Chances had sold my patient file to the highest bidder and that the world now knew about everything that had happened to me the night I turned fifteen.

I'd never revealed the identity of my attacker while I was there, only that somebody had attacked me, but it didn't matter. There were only so many options. I'd attacked Chuck before the HoF in front of just about every major media outlet, and add to that the rumors about Chuck that had existed for decades, and the world quickly put two and two together.

I felt relieved at first, actually. Finally, the truth was out. But then, hearing the events of that night relayed through the television grew horrifying. Everybody in the world now knew exactly what Chuck had done to me, and they learned about it in vivid detail. Everyone put their own little spin on the "breaking news" story, and they were talking about it incessantly. Listening to them, I felt as dirty and ashamed as I did the night it happened.

Then Chuck was on the television, cowering behind his lawyer. No, he wasn't cowering. He was standing there looking fucking indignant and a little bored.

"The release of these records is a fantastic breach of doctor-patient confidentiality," said the lawyer. "My client denies categorically that he is the perpetrator of the horrific crimes laid out in them. Furthermore, given her delicate mental state at the time, it's entirely possible Ms. Moriarty invented the entire episode as a way to deal with her severe substance abuse issues."

I think that's probably when I really ramped up the drinking. Fuck it. If the world was going to think that I'm a drunk, I might as well just go ahead and be a goddamn drunk.

Paparazzi poured into the neighborhood and set up camp just beyond the security gate. The gate buzzer was buzzing incessantly. My phone was ringing. Sara's phone was ringing. I ignored the calls and drank some more. The voices got really loud.

You're lucky your father wanted you!
You're getting more like your father everyday!
Be careful what you wish for, Alice.
You're not her!
Not every fucking thing is about you, Alice.

I grabbed an umbrella from an umbrella stand by the door and pummeled the intercom speaker, over and over again, until it broke open. I grabbed it and ripped the wires from the wall. The buzzing stopped. I did the same thing to the house phone, and then threw my cell on the floor and stomped on it until it broke open. It was silent again.

It felt great to destroy something.

So, I destroyed other things, starting with her gold and platinum albums. I knocked them off the wall one by one, and then stomped on them until there was nothing but pieces left. I smashed all her frames on the wall. I smashed through the liquor bottles on the bar behind her piano and then took aim at the piano itself, pounding the top, over and over again.

Unfortunately for me (and the house), this sent the lit candles on top of it to the floor. They landed beneath the curtains, on the floor that was very, very recently saturated with alcohol. The floor lit up like, well, like it had just been doused with alcohol. The curtains went up a second later.

I continued my destruction. I didn't notice the fire at first, but when I did, I remember being fascinated by the flames. I stopped and just watched them.

That's all I remember.

I woke up a few hours ago in the hospital to the smell of acrid smoke. My mouth was dry and my head throbbed. Not just throbbed. It pulsed. It contracted and expanded, like my brain had turned into a set of lungs in my skull.

Jett was in a chair next to me, slumped over the bed, grasping my hand in his. His hair and clothes were charred. My free hand and forearm were wrapped in gauze, but there was no pain. I glanced up at the IV drip and wondered what kinds of drugs they were pumping into me.

I tested my limbs and was relieved when everything seemed to move properly, and with little pain. My fidgeting roused Jett. He lifted his head, and when his eyes met mine he began to weep. I didn't know what to do. I'd only ever seen Jett cry once, and that was the day he left the house before he and Sara divorced. I'd never seen him openly weep like that. Not even when Sara died.

He bowed his head and touched his face to my hand. "Thank you."

He summoned the doctor and hovered in the back of the room while the doctor examined me. After several rather tedious tests ("can you speak," "watch my light," "squeeze my hand," "can you feel this?"), the doctor spoke to me briefly about my injuries and then left.

He told me I had a moderate concussion, second degree burns on my left arm, and smoke inhalation. At that point, I hadn't even remembered what the hell had happened, so I was very confused.

Jett made his way back to my bed after the doctor left. The right sleeve of his shirt had been sliced off near his shoulder. His upper arm and shoulder were wrapped in gauze and his hair was singed and asymmetrical. He approached me tentatively, which was uncharacteristic of him, and he had a strange look in his eyes.

"You're all burned," I croaked. My throat felt like I'd gargled with barbed wire.

"So are you," he said. His voice was shaky.

"What the hell happened?"

"There was a fire," he said.

"A fire?" I said, thinking back.

Oh, fuck. A fire.

Sara's house.

Jett explained the situation as he understood it. Stuart had called him to tell him that I was all over the television. When he couldn't reach me on my phone, he'd rushed to my apartment to find me. Not finding me there, he'd gone to Sara's house on sheer instinct.

When he got there, flames were coming out of the windows. He'd dashed into the house and pulled me out, burning himself in the process.

He said the umbrella was burning when he got there, and it was still in my hand.

If Jett hadn't gone to Sara's, I'd likely be dead.

They don't know if I passed out from the smoke and hit my head on the way down, or if I tripped trying to flee the house and hit my head then. Nobody will ever know, because I can't remember. I believe it's the latter. From the looks I'm getting around here, though, I'd say general public opinion says I stood by and let the smoke overtake me.

"How long have I been out?" I asked.

Jett checked his wrist out of habit but found only skin where his watch should have been. He thought back a moment and then glanced at the clock on the wall.

"About five and a half hours," he said. "They said it was a good sign if you woke up within six."

He was crying again. I understood then what that look was in his eyes. It was guilt.

"Why didn't you tell me, Alice?" he asked, sniffling. "Why didn't you tell me about Wall?"

I shrugged.

"You could have told me, you know," said Jett. "I would have put an end to it."

"You'd have put an end to him, you mean," I said. "And you would have been in jail. Then who would I have had?"

I was crying then, too. There was a lot of very not-rock-star-like crying that night.

"How's the house?" I asked when our blubbering had subsided.

"Still burning, last I knew," said Jett, wiping his eyes. "The fire is contained, but it looks to be a total loss."

Whoops.

"Where's everybody else?" I asked.

Jett hesitated, and I knew it was bad news.

"What's going on?" I pressed.

"Your father is in the county jail," said Jett. "Stuart is out doing the media rounds, trying to keep us ahead of this thing while I work to get Stephen out on bail, and Alfie is M.I.A."

Jett bowed his head and thumbed the skin between his eyes. Overworked, manager Jett was returning, and it was a welcome return. Weeping Jett was too heartbreaking to handle for very long.

"Why's Stephen in jail?"

I assumed he'd been busted for drinking and driving or something, but the truth was much better, or worse, depending on your perspective on the situation.

After Chuck's press conference, Stephen went to Chuck's home and waited for him. When Chuck got there, Stephen pulled him out of his car and beat the hell out of him, right there in front of the dozens of photographers, who had also gathered outside Chuck's house to wait for him.

I watched the videos online a few minutes ago. They're damning evidence, to be sure, against Stephen, should his case end up at trial. I can't help feeling some pride when I watch them though, and, if I'm honest, a deep satisfaction. The headlines scream things like, "Stephen Moriarty attacks record producer Chuck Wall," but to me, it is my dad attacking the scumbag who abused me, and I can't bring myself to wish he hadn't done it, even knowing he could end up in prison because of it.

Stephen beat him so badly, Chuck ended up in the hospital; this hospital, actually. His room is just one floor below me. I haven't decided yet if I'll pay him a visit. All I can envision when I think about doing that is me holding a pillow over his face until he stops breathing, so I suppose I should just skip it.

We'll see.

HE NEEDS YOU
—October 6, 2010

I dreamed of Sara while I was asleep. I just remembered. It was so surreal. Obviously. Dreams always are, but this was different. I won't go as far as to say it was a don't-go-into-the-light moment, but I won't say it wasn't either.

In the dream, I woke up on the floor of the Great Room and the smoke and heat were gone. The room was bright, much brighter than it had ever been in reality; not only brighter but cleaner. Fresher. Brand new light, maybe.

Sara was playing "Little One" on her piano. I walked to her and listened to her play, just listened. I wasn't sure if she was even aware of me at first, but then she stopped and looked at me. We looked at each other for a very long time.

She gestured to the flowers that sat in a delicate, crystal vase at the center of the piano. It was a bouquet of lilies, her favorite.

"They're beautiful, aren't they?" said Sara, her voice an echo.

I nodded.

Standing, Sara walked around the piano and plucked one of the lilies from the vase, snipping its stem. She tucked the flower behind my ear and fussed a little with my hair. When she was finished, she put her hands on my shoulders, examining her work.

"There," she said. "Perfect."

She was the age she would have been today, Diary, but she was no longer a tortured soul. She looked refreshed and at peace. Youthful. Brand new, like the light.

It had never been easy for me to see her so sad, as she was so often when I was a kid. I remember that now. My anger has overshadowed many things for me for so much of my life, but I remember it now, how devastating it was to see her in so much pain.

This Sara, this Sara was the one she was supposed to be. The one she would have been, in a different world.

"He needs you, you know," said Sara.

My eyebrows furrowed. "Who?"

But she only smiled and brought her hands to either side of my face. "Go now."

The next moment, I woke up in the hospital.

It was a goodbye. I understand that now. I understand that I'll never see her again. For all she was and wasn't to me, it makes me sad.

I can't stop crying.

LILY
—October 7, 2010

Alfie visited me tonight. I was drifting in and out of sleep, and when I opened my eyes, he was there in the doorway, leaning against it. I'm starting to think he has an underlying suspicion about the stability of all doorways.

"It's not polite to stare," I squeaked.

My larynx was damaged by smoke inhalation. The doctors are cautiously optimistic that it isn't permanent. They say if I rest my voice and quit smoking cigarettes, I should heal fine. I think Jett paid them to give me the second part of those instructions.

Anyhow, Alfie came into my room. He pulled a chair to the bed and sat, handing me some flowers. Lilies. I stuck my nose into them and sniffed. I couldn't smell them—my sinuses were also damaged by the smoke—but I'm sure they smelled nice.

"Thanks," I said.

"You're welcome."

Sara had filled her house with lilies, always. Even in her worst times there were always lilies around.

It made sense now.

"That would have been her name," I said. It was a statement, not a question.

He blinked. "What?"

"Lily," I said. "That would have been her name."

"Yes," he said, eyeing me sidelong. "How did you know that?"

"I had a dream," I said and then laughed because it sounded so ridiculous.

My "laugh" was more like the bark of a seal, and the sound made me laugh more. That sent me into a coughing fit. Alfie popped up and poured me some water from the carafe next to the bed. I waved it off.

"Drink," he said.

"Thanks," I croaked, sipping it.

He settled back into his chair and stared down into his lap. When he looked up his eyes were wet.

Sad, sexy Alfie returns!

"You had a dream?" he said.

"I had a something," I said, shrugging. "Sara was there, and she had lilies too."

His eyes filled with more tears as he listened and he looked down again, fiddling with the rings on his fingers.

"We, uh, we never knew about the baby, the baby we lost, until it was gone." He cleared his throat. "But we'd discussed names in the past, children's names, just in passing, really. Lily was a frontrunner for a girl child."

"Is she the Little One?" I asked.

"You both are, I guess," he said, closing his eyes. "It all happened so fast. You were born only about six months after she would have been," said Alfie, sniffing. He wiped his nose with his sleeve like a little boy. "The line between you and her has always been a bit blurred in my mind."

It explained so much: why he's despised me my whole life. It wasn't because I broke up the band or ruined what he had with Sara. It was because I wasn't her. My existence reminded him that his daughter never got the chance to live.

I wonder if that's why Sara hated me too. Would she have loved Lily? Would she have been a mother to Alfie's child?

He was crying then. Full on crying! For Christ's sake, if people don't quit crying around me, I'm going to develop a complex. Another complex. I imagine there will be tears from Stephen, too. Those I can handle—those I might even relish, to be honest—but I swear to God, if Stuart drops by and starts bawling, I'm moving to Canada or Antarctica or somewhere.

SCARS
—November 13, 2010

Jett and I went to her house yesterday. What's left of her house, anyhow.

Man, I really did a number on that thing. The guest houses and pool house survived, and so did the garages, but the main house was nothing but a scorched shell, like the carcass of a beached whale, plopped down right there in the middle of Laurel Canyon.

"I can't believe I burned it down," I muttered.

"Your father nearly burned our hotel down once," said Jett.

I turned to him to respond, but he was walking so close behind me that we ran right into each other.

"Oh, sorry," he said.

"Dude!" I said, grabbing his shoulders. "We need to discuss this whole mother hen thing you've got going on lately."

"Mother hen thing?" he asked.

"Yes!" I said. "I appreciate it. I really do. You're looking out for me, and that's great. But you have got to give me a little bit of space, or I'm going to snap."

He held up his hands and took a few, dramatic steps back.

"Thank you," I said. "Where were we?"

"Your father almost burning down our hotel," said Jett.

"Oh, right," I said. "He did?"

"Mmm hmm. In Berlin, a few years before the wall fell. It's the reason we're not allowed in Germany anymore."

"We're not allowed in Germany?"

"Well, you can probably get in, but Wonderland has been banned from performing there since the mid-eighties," he said. "In fact, if you're looking to escape your mother hen, that'd be a good place to go."

"Ha ha," I said, turning back to the house.

The landing of the patio was about as close as we could get to the house. What was left of the front door was cordoned off with police tape. We'd been told by the police that their official investigation was complete, but I wasn't risking anything by breaching their tape.

According to the nice lady at the homeowner's insurance company, which has already refused to pay a dime to rebuild the house, I'm lucky I'm not going to jail for arson. I don't really think that's for her to say, but whatever. She's not wrong. I think I'm actually pretty lucky I didn't burn down the whole neighborhood. Los Angeles is pretty, fucking dry these days.

I stood on the landing and peaked inside the front door, which had been hacked through by a fireman's ax. The door hung precariously on only one hinge.

"Hey, my statues survived!" I said.

My stoic, old marble pals were the only recognizable things inside. They maintained their watch over the charred mess around them.

Jett yanked on the police tape and ripped it off the door. Apparently, he wasn't worried about the police.

"What are you doing?" I said.

"A crew will be here in the morning to demolish what's left and take away the wreckage," he said, clasping his hands behind his back. He looked one of the statues up and down, sizing it up. They stood almost eye to eye—two protectors facing off. "We should salvage your friends, don't you think?"

I smiled.

We tried to move them ourselves but, as it turns out, solid marble statues are not easily moved by humans. Jett called the wrecking crew and told them that the statues were to be salvaged and then called a moving company and left instructions to deliver the statues to his house.

I don't know how he does it. I don't think he even looked up any phone numbers. He just seemed to know them.

I really think Jett might know everything.

I sat on the front step and gingerly scratched the healing skin on my arm. It had been itching relentlessly for about a week, since the pain of the burns had worn off. The doctors said I should have minimal scarring. That is, if I quit scratching at it.

Jett sat next to me, tucking away his phone. He sighed when he noticed me scratching and put his good hand over mine. "I swear, I will tape oven mitts over your hands if you don't quit that."

I grumbled and stopped.

We looked out over the scorched earth at the foot of the patio and the lawn beyond it. It was a hazy day. The notorious L.A. smog drifted between the hills in the distance.

"God, I hated this place," I said.

"I know," he said.

"Jesus, I didn't mean to burn it down, though," I muttered.

"I know that, too," said Jett.

"There was so much history here..." I said.

There really was. A lot of it was bad, of course, at least from my perspective, but, history-wise, materialistically-speaking, I destroyed some pretty valuable things.

Her gold and platinum albums were smashed and burned. Her clothes; her shoes; her hats and other accessories, they were all gone. The Hall of Fame or Hard Rock Cafe probably wouldn't have minded getting their hands on that stuff. Thankfully, I'd had her trunk of journals shipped to my apartment, or those would be gone too.

I haven't gone through those yet. I'm not sure I ever will.

"Why didn't you ever tell me about Lily?" I asked.

Jett considered a moment. "Would it have helped you?"

It was my turn to consider. "I suppose not."

My skin began to itch again. When I scratched it, Jett shook his head and muttered something about how he hoped I enjoyed my scars.

"I've started to think of her as my sister," I said.

Jett looked at me. "Lily?"

"Mmm hmm," I said, nodding. "Weird, right?"

Jett shrugged. "Not so weird."

But it was weird. I can't help it, though. I've even started asking her advice about things. Lily's become yet another voice in my head.

Rumors of a *Wonderland* curse at The Hollywood Bowl are spreading like wildfire (pun intended) around the net, since Sara died right after a show there, and I almost died right before one. Both tours were abruptly suspended. This must mean we're cursed, obviously.

It couldn't possibly just mean that we're really fucked up.

Some people have way too much time on their hands.

"Have you heard anything about the tour?" I asked.

Jett scoffed. "Fuck the tour."

"Language!"

Of course, he had a point. Stephen might be going to jail. It'll be weeks before we know if I'll even be able to sing again. Alfie is probably still curled up in a ball somewhere crying. It's not the best time to discuss heading back out on the road.

"They can sue, for all I care," said Jett. "They can sue us and take all our money. I don't care. All I really want to do right now is take a fucking nap."

Oh boy. Jett hadn't taken a nap in thirty years.

"You're starting to sound like me," I said.

"Have you spoken to your father?" he asked after a few minutes a silence.

"No," I said, though I knew he already knew the answer to his question. "Not yet."

"I think he'd really like to see you," said Jett.

"Yeah," I said.

There were a lot of things I would have liked in my life too. A functioning father, for one.

"Yeah, I'll get there," I said. "I just...haven't yet."

In my peripheral, Jett held out his hands, palms up, but this time, he didn't move them when I slapped at them. Instead, he grabbed my hands, squeezing gently.

"You're going to be okay, you know," he said.

I nodded, but I wasn't entirely convinced.

"All right. Come on, Cherrio," he said. "It's getting late. Buy you a birthday dinner?"

He helped me up, and we walked to his car.

I turned back and looked at the house one last time. It was the last time I would ever see it, and that was an oddly sad notion to me. Sure, I could rebuild, eventually, but it wouldn't be the same.

I thought then that I'd probably miss the house.

And I wouldn't say this to anybody but you, Diary, but I thought then that I would probably miss her, too.

Yes, Sara should have been a better mother to me. I know that. The drugs that eventually killed her, and her inability to see beyond Alfie, robbed me of a mother.

But I'm just one person. Millions loved her, and she loved them back. She saved lives with her music. Her words comforted millions of people in their darkest hours. Maybe that will have to be enough for me.

Because Sara wasn't heartless. She had a lot of love to give; she just didn't have any left for me.

I don't know. I'll figure it out, I suppose.

I think I'm going to take a break from writing to you, Diary. I need to get outside of my head for a while. Today is my twenty-second birthday, and sometimes it feels like I've been inside my head the entire twenty-two years. That wouldn't necessarily be a bad thing if I could learn to recognize my voice among the many in there and ignore the rest. Because the rest of them are assholes.

Except for Lily. She's okay.

I won't be gone long.

AFTERWORD

This project has been many years in the making. The story formed in my mind during the summer before my freshman year of college. It was a tumultuous time for me, and I think that particular summer is a tumultuous time for anybody—leaving the sheltering bubble of high school and all the emotions that go along with that. This story was my way of escaping what was going on around me, I think.

It was only a shell of a story then, and barely that. It had no real characters or plot; only vague personality types and a general premise. I was set to begin my college studies, working for a degree in physical education and health. I thought I would become a teacher. I had no idea the story was headed anywhere other than the confines of my mind. Nearly nineteen years later, it's a completed novel and set to be released out into the world.

I'm not exactly sure how I feel right now. Happy, for sure; excited. I'm certainly proud to have completed this project. My old friend anxiety seems to be the over-riding emotion as I write this. I'm not sure there will ever come a time when the anxiety goes away completely. In fact, I hope that time never comes. Pushing past the fear is what has gotten me to this point, and I'm quite happy to be here.

Thank you for reading.

ABOUT THE AUTHOR

After earning college degrees in fields that gave her little satisfaction, Kristen Skeet decided to dedicate her time to her first love: writing. She's been published in *The Buffalo News* and has written novels and short stories. Kristen is a film buff and music fanatic, enjoys bicycling and hiking, and is also an avid traveler. The greatest film of all time is Jurassic Park, and she will argue her case with anybody who disagrees. Kristen has followed Fleetwood Mac around the world since 1997 and is convinced she'd be a millionaire by now if only she had saved the money she's spent on concert tickets, flights, and drinks at airport bars. But what fun would that be? Her favorite cities to visit are Dublin, Toronto, and New York City. Kristen currently lives in Western New York with her tuxedo cat, Max.

www.kristenskeet.com